SPIES AND WEDDINGS

CONNOR WHITELEY

No part of this book may be reproduced in any form or by any electronic or mechanical means. Including information storage, and retrieval systems, without written permission from the author except for the use of brief quotations in a book review.

This book is NOT legal, professional, medical, financial or any type of official advice.

Any questions about the book, rights licensing, or to contact the author, please email connorwhiteley@connorwhiteley.net

Copyright © 2023 CONNOR WHITELEY

All rights reserved.

DEDICATION
Thank you to all my readers without you I couldn't do what I love.

CHAPTER 1

To MI5 Officer Alfie Stewart, the only problem with being an intelligence officer that was betrayed, having his identity exposed and being doomed to spend the rest of his life behind a desk was that he was thousands or hundreds of miles away from the beautiful love of his life, Louis.

But that was always the price of love and being an intelligence officer at the same time.

Alfie stood staring out of the slightly dirty and rain splattered floor-to-ceiling windows that gave him an amazing view that overlooked London with its tall skyscrapers, stunning cathedrals and immensely tall bridges, in his office.

Alfie had always preferred to be out in the world, spying on the UK's enemies and enjoying the occasional male enemy that Alfie just had to sleep with for the sake of the mission, at least that's how he justified it at the time and it was before he met Louis anyway, but now he was just stuck to live out his doomed career in a corner office.

It wasn't exactly the worst of offices in all of MI5, at least it was a large rectangular office with bright white walls that Alfie hung decorative landscapes, there was a great oak desk with his computer, classified files and other intelligence reports on top. It was rather nice in a way and Alfie seriously never wanted to work in the "bull pen" with all the younger agents again.

He really didn't need to hear about their latest sexual conquests and how many women they had slept with on different missions.

That was probably the very last thing Alfie was actually interested in.

The wonderful hints of lavender, roses and lilacs made Alfie smile as the aromas radiated across the office from a freshly bought Parisian vase filled with the stunning flowers that Louis had sent him.

Alfie might not have been allowed to know what or where or even when Louis's missions took place but it was amazing and a real testament to their love that Louis sent him so many gifts of his travels, as Alfie was officially banned from international travel.

The gentle sound of a cleaner hoovering made Alfie want to start looking at some Iran intelligence reports that his best friend, Penelope Pimple, had delivered to him earlier, but he just hated being stuck in his awful office for the rest of his life.

And it was all because an idiot ex-boyfriend intelligence officer had sold his story to the media.

When Alfie had first met MI6 agent Sebastian Crawford, the sheer pompousness of the name should have told him everything he needed to know, Alfie had found the beautiful man charming, witty and so sensationally sexy that it really hadn't taken much to make Alfie want to have sex with the man.

Even though a year later, it turned out Sebastien was only using him for his own gains, not even the gains of MI6, so Alfie was walking to work one day and found he was on the front page of every local, national and international newspaper telling of all the operations he had been involved in, who he had an hadn't killed and most importantly the classified details of a major op he was working on at that time.

Which of course MI6 quickly took over and they got all the credit for the operation. Alfie really hated them.

Alfie was still rather surprised that he hadn't been "let go" or imprisoned or whatever, and he was even more surprised that Sebastien had never been released from MI6, in fact he was now leading a major international counterfeiting department of agents.

So despite him compromising national security, destroying a bunch of political relationships and earning over a million pounds (the price of selling the stories to the papers), his career had skyrocketed and Alfie's had died.

Someone knocked on Alfie's office's glass door.

Alfie looked and smiled when it saw that it was Penelope, and she really did look beautiful today with her long blond hair, long flowing black dress that only highlighted her stunning slim figure and her model-like face was so perfect, considering she was getting married later tonight.

"Why are you still here?" Alfie asked, waving her in and hugging her.

Penelope smiled. "You know I love my job and I'm not getting married until nine o'clock tonight, that's eight hours away, because of the security checks, there was a bomb scare at the venue and... my father was shot at today,"

Alfie just nodded, because to normal people that might have sounded strange and rather exciting. But if there was one thing Alfie had learnt about the Pimple family in recent years, it was that they might have been some of the UK's top spies, but they were very, very accident prone.

And given how Penelope was the daughter of the deputy director of MI5, and her mother was the head of MI6, the security checks were always going to be very vast and almost ridiculous, and it didn't exactly help that a number of senior politicians were going from both the Government and Opposition parties.

"And as your Supervisor," Penelope said, "I actually do have to ask about the Iran reports. Have you looked at them yet?"

Alfie shrugged. "Can I just say how beautiful you are?"

Penelope laughed and playfully hit Alfie on the head. "Get the reports done please before the wedding and I go off on my honeymoon, and I spoke to DGSE and they confirmed Louis is travelling back to London tonight,"

That was amazing news, and Alfie was more than glad he finally knew that Louis had been working with the French secret service on something. But just the idea of seeing beautiful, sexy Louis again made Alfie's hands go sweaty, his stomach filled with butterflies and his head almost went light.

Penelope's phone buzzed. "Oh,"

"What?" Alfie asked.

"Beautiful," Penelope said, "you have a visitor from MI6,"

Alfie rolled his eyes. "What is it your father again wanting to make sure I don't cock-up the speech?"

Penelope laughed. "No but that is one of his top concerns about the wedding,"

Alfie just glared at her, Alfie had been working so hard for the wedding over the past few months with wedding prep, decorating and conducting background checks on all five hundred guests. He wasn't going to cock-up his best friend's wedding speech.

He hoped.

"Sebastian Crawford is coming up to see you," Penelope said as she quickly left the office.

Alfie just stood there feeling numb. Why the hell was his dickhead of an ex here?

CHAPTER 2

The absolutely stunning aromas of sea salt, fish and chips and freshly opened white wine filled the sea air as MI5 officer Louis O'Deal leant against the icy cold railings of the ferry as it travelled between Calais in France and Dover, England.

Louis loved the long metal ferry with its white metal floor and hull with so many English, French and other Europeans packed so tightly together that Louis was sure it wouldn't be hard for an assassin to knock into their victim and kill someone without them even noticing, the real problem would be the assassin escaping, but that was just his intelligence mind working in overdrive again.

Louis was surrounded by little young families that had just returned from holidaying in France, and that kept saying how wonderful the country was, its people were and how sensational the food was.

Louis couldn't agree more, and he really loved English people going over to France to see what it was really like, instead of believing all the lies about France. Because the French people were so kind, supportive and fun that Louis was still surprised how the DGSE agents he had met had given him a tour around Paris, and actually listened to his suggestions.

It was a very nice change from all the elderly MI5 snobs that refused to listen to him because Louis was only 29 and been an agent for nine years, instead of their 40 or whatever.

Louis had really enjoyed the mission to hunt down an extremist white supremacy group of English nutters in Paris, but all Louis wanted to do now was go home, see Alfie and hopefully have a quick shag before the wedding.

He might have only been away from the love of his life for a week, it honestly felt like years and Louis really, really missed him. He missed running his hands through Alfie's longish brown hair that framed his amazingly cute face so perfectly, and Louis really missed kissing Alfie's skinny fit body.

Louis just smiled to himself as the ferry went up and down in the choppy waters and the young families around him laughed as a little boy wobbled slightly and fell on Louis.

So Louis just helped him up and the mother thanked him, before the salty air picked up and blew harder and harder, so the young families tried to hurry inside (not that there was any room inside) to get out of the horrible weather.

"You're welcome," Louis said.

Louis didn't mind the strong salty air blowing past his cheeks and coating his skin in a very thin layer of salt, the salty smell was a very nice contrast from the sheer heat and cleanliness of Paris and much of the other places in France that he had travelled to in the past week.

Even the terrorists and white supremacists' apartments seemed remarkably clean considering hygiene was never normally in their skill set, but Louis was really looking forward to the wedding.

He had known Penelope and the rest of the Pimple family a lot longer than beautiful Alfie had, even though Alfie had first met Penelope at university, and he was really glad that Penelope had found someone special.

It was even better that Penelope's boyfriend, Adrian Lordheart, was bi and Louis could thankfully confirm that Adrian was a great guy both in bed and outside of it, he was kind, helpful and really cared about the people in his life.

Louis and Adrian were still friends and they talked at least once a week, recently it had mainly been about wedding preparation, whilst beautiful Alfie and Penelope talked about it from their side of it all, and even now Louis was still surprised at how good Alfie was at the more feminine and girly side of traditional weddings.

Not that the Pimples were traditionalists in the slightest and things were never simple with them.

Penelope and Adrian could have been married

months ago if the Pimples had simply ordered the wedding to be on a country estate that was always secured for foreign diplomatic visits. Security was perfect there, but no, the Pimple just had to have it at their country estate and that all kicked off the rather long process of security checks and more.

As the white cliffs of Dover started to light up the horizon, Louis felt his stomach flip in excitement as he was finally going to be back in England and then finally he could see the love of his life beautiful Alfie.

And then Louis could hopefully slip into his wedding suit and meet Alfie at the wedding venue.

The only problem with that plan was given how beautiful Alfie looked anyway he was going to look even better in a suit. So the problem was Louis was definitely going to struggle not to jump Alfie there and then at the wedding.

It was going to be a massive struggle indeed.

CHAPTER 3

Of all the people that Alfie had ever expected to walk into his office, including assassins, maybe a jealous girlfriend from his straight period or even a former military soldier looking for revenge (the reason behind that is strictly top-secret), Alfie never ever guessed that Sebastian Crawford would dare to show himself again.

It was hardly a secret that everyone in MI5 hated the man, but just because of that, Alfie didn't want Sebastian to feel endangered. Not now. So Alfie simply sat on his large black chair at his oak desk, turned off his computers and hid the intelligence reports so MI6 couldn't steal anything else from him, and simply waited.

Alfie was almost tempted to abandon the Parisian vase filled with the stunning flowers were they were, but Alfie quickly moved them so they were the only thing on the desk. At least that way Sebastian would know that Alfie was happily in a relationship and he had moved on from all the crap that he had pulled.

And the most important thing was that Alfie just needed to remain calm, and definitely not attack his traitorous, awful ex-boyfriend that had cost him so much.

"In there sir," an elderly woman said that was Penelope's secretary as she pointed Sebastian into Alfie's office.

Alfie instantly hated Sebastian's tall, muscular frame with his wonderful broad shoulders, great-looking body and his killer smile. He had a slight blondish beard now that Alfie wasn't exactly sure he liked, but Sebastian definitely looked amazing in his three-piece suit that made him look like he was from the English Nobility, and not some poor kid that grew up on a council estate in some dying city in the north of England.

Sebastian smiled and extended his hand towards Alfie as he sat down on one of the two very comfortable blue fabric chairs in front of the desk.

Alfie didn't even stand up to shake his hand.

"Be quick," Alfie said.

"Now, now, surely we can have an honest and gentle conversation," he said.

Alfie just laughed. That was seriously not going to happen even if Sebastian hadn't destroyed his career.

"What do you want? I have intelligence reports to review, a boyfriend to see and a wedding to attend to," Alfie said.

Sebastian bowed his head slightly as if he was mocking Alfie. "I am glad you found love again after me. I just really hoped I didn't hurt you too much but a profit is a profit and business is just business,"

Alfie laughed. "At least I finally know that I was only business and easy sex for you,"

"You were definitely easy but I like to-"

Alfie waved him silent. "What do you want?"

Sebastian smiled and started touching the soft silky leaves and petals of Louis' flowers, and Alfie forced himself not to break Sebastian's wrist.

"I want what all spies and husbands want," Sebastian said. "My boyfriend and me are getting married,"

Alfie shrugged. "Good for you, now get out of my life,"

Sebastian started playing more and more with the petals and then Alfie realised that Sebastian Crawford of all people was actually nervous.

Alfie had never ever seen Sebastian nervous in all the time he had unfortunately known him, he was never scared or concerned or worried, so why was he nervous now?

"My boyfriend says the only way he would only marry me is if you attend the wedding,"

Alfie smiled. That was not what he was expecting in the slightest, and if anything, it sounded a little dodgy and just flat out weird.

"Only marry you if I was there?" Alfie asked.

"Why? Do I know the man?"

Sebastian shrugged. "I don't know. Ever heard of Louie Carter from Counterterrorism,"

Alfie shook his head, this was beyond weird though, and in his experience as an intelligence officer, before Sebastian destroyed his career, if something felt odd then there were only two routes.

Run like hell. Run into the fire.

"Ask me then," Alfie said smiling.

Sebastian bit his lip. "Alfie I would like you to attend my wedding,"

"No," Alfie said, laughing.

Sebastian's face dropped and his eyes wettened, and then Alfie realised that this wasn't a lie by Sebastian. His boyfriend was deadly serious about it being a requirement to marry him.

Alfie bit his lip and he really, really didn't want to go, but it would be interesting to meet this Louie Carter, and ask him what the hell he saw in traitorous Sebastian. And it would be an absolutely perfect excuse to see stunning Louis in his sexy suit.

Alfie's office door flew open. Penelope rushed in.

"Massive problem, wedding's cancelled," Penelope said. "Iranian terrorists have bombed the venue, taken five caterers as hostage and are threatening to attack my family's country estate. Bye,"

Then Penelope simply rushed out of the office.

Alfie just looked at Sebastian. "When's your wedding then?"

CHAPTER 4

Louis went into the living room of his and Alfie's large London penthouse apartment with its wonderful black sofa, dark wooden coffee table and two single recliner chairs opposite each other, all surrounded by stunning built-in white bookcases, and Louis was rather shocked at what he saw.

As much as he loved seeing Alfie in a black silky dressing gown that seriously highlighted how fit he was, utterly beautiful his face was and how perfectly relaxed he was just laying there on the sofa reading some intelligence reports, Louis hadn't expected to see him at all.

The traffic from Dover to London had been awful and the wedding was meant to start in less than an hour, surely both of them should be getting ready and prepared for their best friends' wedding?

"Wedding's cancelled. Pimple style reasons," Alfie said as he got up and walked over to Louis.

Louis just smiled and nodded. He knew he would

get the full details later but he was hardly surprised that there was probably some sort of bombing, terrorists and other things involved in a Pimple family affair, he actually would have been upset if there wasn't.

But Louis was really looking forward to seeing Alfie in his wedding suit that highlighted everything so well, and it would have been great to see Alfie being so happy, laughing and smiling at Penelope's wedding after everything he had had to deal with.

Louis just wanted Alfie to be happy.

Louis wrapped his arms round Alfie's small beautiful body as they kissed and Louis seriously loved and missed and treasured the amazing taste and feeling of Alfie's soft lips against his. Then Alfie broke away and went back to sitting on the sofa, making sure he was very conservatively covered up.

Louis wasn't sure what was going on but something was clearly up, because in the years he had loved Alfie, he had never covered himself up so much, and Louis was sure Alfie was even embarrassed to be wearing a silky dressing gown in the first place.

Louis gently went over to the Sofa and hugged Alfie, and was rather surprised when Alfie immediately rested his head on his shoulder, and sat there in silence.

Louis had no clue what would have bothered him so much. It definitely wasn't jealous of him being allowed out on missions when Alfie wasn't, because they had overcome that battle and extremely soar wound early on in their relationship (with very interesting fights before then), it couldn't be because Louis's mission had meant they were a part of a week, because they both understand that at a deep level and Louis had been away for months before.

Louis just didn't know what it could be.

"What's wrong?" Louis asked.

The silence in the living room was broken for a few seconds by the loud sound of people thundering down the corridor outside and banging on doors before they ran away, and Louis hadn't missed those boys.

"Sebastian came to see me," Alfie said.

Louis sat up perfectly straight. "Are you okay? Are you hurt? Do I need to contact my friends in the DGSE to blackmail Sebastian?"

Alfie just sat up and cocked his head. "The DGSE have material on him?"

Louis knew he had made a little mistake there but he shrugged. "And MI5 and 6 have material on them, we are spies after all,"

Alfie nodded. "Okay but, no he didn't hurt me. He wanted me to go to his wedding,"

Louis wanted to laugh, hiss or do some kind of disproving gesture but Alfie seemed to be at least considering this. Louis wasn't sure if this was a type of thing he needed to support or not.

Alfie moved a large pile of intelligence reports from the sofa, that Louis hadn't realised was there, onto the coffee table and Louis loved it that Alfie laid down on the sofa with his beautiful little head in his lap.

Louis gently played with his hair. "Do you want to go?"

"I know you're being careful and all, but what do you think?" Alfie asked.

"Why does he want you there?" Louis asked.

"He says his boyfriend won't marry him unless I'm there. Do you know agent Louie Carter Counter terrorism?"

Louie nodded. "Of course, I worked with him a few months back but… I'll show you,"

Louie took out his black smartphone, entered a bunch of passwords and bought up Carter's file with pictures and showed them to Alfie. Louie did have to admit that Carter was cute because he was a very typical twink in a way, with his very young and smooth body that Carter had promised Louie came in very handy on missions.

And Carter had a very youthful face, very well-done makeup and Louie could only really describe him as looking like a twelve-year-old boy with beautifully done make-up and hair.

"He's a 12-year-old," Alfie said harshly. "He's marrying a 12-year-old beautiful boy and I'm…"

Louie just smiled. "You're what?"

Alfie looked at and Louie just stared into those beautiful eyes.

"And I'm here on a sofa with the love of my life who is the most beautiful man I've ever seen,"

Louie playfully pulled his hair. "Good save, but it's that reaction that means you're still having problems with Sebastian,"

Alfie stood up and went to the other side of the coffee table. Louie almost felt like the coffee table was a barrier between them, it might as well have been Sebastian himself.

"Of course I have problems with him," Alfie said. "He's a dickhead agent who ruined by life and my career and my love life. You know before I met you and all. I still have trust problems,"

Louie nodded. It made sense and it was a pain something that Alfie would hesitate in telling him things even though they had been together for so long.

Louie went over to Alfie and kissed him. "If you need to go to the wedding to put your feelings about Sebastian to bed, then we will go,"

Alfie looked unsure and went to look at the ground but Louie raised Alfie's beautiful chin and kissed him again.

"You would go with me?" Alfie asked.

Louie laughed. "Of course. I have a feeling our relationship will always have baggage attached if you and Sebastian don't sort each other out,"

When Alfie slowly nodded and just hugged him, Louie really wasn't sure how helpful that comment had been, but it didn't matter.

Because no matter what he was there for beautiful Alfie and he was certain that Louie and Alfie could never take their relationship to the next level (which at his point was marriage) if Alfie didn't deal with this painful past.

And Louie just wanted to support him. No matter where that pain led them.

Then Alfie simply dropped his silky black dressing gown to the floor.

CHAPTER 5

A few hours later after a particularly great session, Alfie just laid on his and Louis's king size bed with its thin blue silk sheets, soft but supportive pillows and the cold metal of their guns (for protection of course) sent little chills up Alfie's arm as he rested his fingers on it.

It wasn't like he expected to be attacked in his own home and he certainly didn't expect something to jump out at him in the pitch darkness of his bedroom, but for the first time in ages, he really, really missed his old life.

Back when he was an intelligence officer, life was so simple because he was an MI5 officer travelling all around the UK, stopping criminals and terrorists and keeping the amazing people of the UK safe, all without them knowing the dangers that could have ended with immense pain.

But now Alfie was just stuck behind his desk, looking at intelligence reports and helping other agents do the job he should be doing. Sure Louis had told him plenty of times that Alfie was the best analyst he had worked with, his job was important and the rest of it. But surely as his boyfriend Louis had to say all those things?

No one else had ever hinted that Alfie's work was important, or as critical as his intelligence work had been.

And whilst Alfie truly loved the feeling of Louis's strong arms wrapped protectively and lovingly around him, he just couldn't forget or stop thinking about that awful thing that Louis had said to him earlier.

Something about the two of them couldn't be perfectly happy until he had dealt with his past of Sebastian.

That couldn't be true in the slightest, Alfie had come so far in his relationship with Louis. Alfie trusted him a lot, not completely so there was a little way to go, Alfie loved Louis more than he loved anyone else in the entire world. So that was surely progress because until he met Louis Alfie doubted he could ever do that again.

But something still felt so wrong.

And then Alfie realised that Louis didn't have as much of a past as he did, and he was sound sleep in an intelligence officer sort of way so the slightest sound of danger would wake him up, but at least Louis was sleeping instead of being awake at this ungodly hour thinking about all the damage a jumped-up MI6 agent had done all those years ago.

Alfie just shook his head and really knew he had to call Penelope, if anyone could help him figure this out it was definitely his best friend in the entire world.

So Alfie carefully removed Louis's amazing sexy arms and didn't even bother to put clothes on as he silently slipped out of the bedroom with his smartphone into the living room of their apartment.

Alfie dialled.

As the phone dialled he leant on the cold, against his skin, black sofa and rested his feet up on the wooden coffee table and he just focused on the large pieces of (fake) art of a forest landscape on one of the walls as the phone rang.

Penelope finally answered. "Hi Al,"

The sound of gun firing and the shouting of Arabic and the screaming of people in the background of Penelope's voice made Alfie a little interested.

"Everything okay?"

"Oh yea totally," Penelope said, sounding like she was firing a gun.

"What's all the shooting?"

Penelope hissed. "Damn it he shot at me. Oh yea, me and dad and mum got a tip off on the Iranians who bombed our country estate so we're raiding their safehouse. Tons of them,"

More bullets screamed down the phone. Alfie was about to grab his gun, coat and Louis when Penelope sounded like she was punching something.

"You okay?" Alfie asked.

Penelope laughed. "Of course. I just snapped a terrorist's neck. What you need?"

Alfie was almost tempted to hang up but the Pimple family might have been nightmares about organising things but they were legendary spies.

Penelope could handle a little conversation and fighting.

"Louis said we can't be happy together until I put my past with Sebastian behind me,"

"Bastard," Penelope said as more bullets smashed into something. "Bloody scum made me chip a nail,"

Alfie really wanted to be there with her but he forced himself to stay.

"He is right beaut," Penelope said sounding like her high-heels were echoing on concrete.

"Why? I love Louis. I'm happy with him and-"

"And it's midnight and you're on-" Penelope said as she punched something. "Sorry about that. You're on the phone with me instead of sleeping with your boyfriend,"

That was unfair and Alfie couldn't believe that everyone seemed to know him far better than he knew himself.

"Not true. I simply had a lot on my mind," Alfie said, failing to even convince himself.

"Stop!" Penelope shouted down the phone and it sounded like she started running.

Moments later three gunshots went off and the line went dead.

Alfie sat up perfectly straight waiting for the phone to ring again.

She couldn't be dead. Alfie needed his best friend more than anything. Alfie couldn't be a person without her amazing support.

Still nothing.

Alfie heard Louis stir from their bedroom but it didn't matter. He just needed to make sure Penelope was okay.

Still nothing.

Alfie couldn't believe she was dead. He had no idea who he was going to play bridge with, mock the other agents with or watch silly films that Louis hated with.

Alfie's phone rang from a different number. He answered it.

"Bloody Iranians," Penelope said. "Bloody shot my phone but don't worry. I pounded his head in. Now Al where were we?"

Alfie heard their bedroom open. "Where you told me that my life isn't being ruled by Sebastian's damage?"

"Wrap it up Penny. Iranian Embassy guys will be here in five," a man said away from the phone.

Alfie just knew that was her dad.

"Can't talk now," Penelope said. "But Al, go to the wedding. Louis is right. And just know I've rescheduled mine to a week tomorrow,"

Penelope hung up.

Alfie just put the phone down and he had to

admit that was probably one of the weirdest phone calls he had ever had to make in his little life.

"What was that?" Louis asked, very tired and he really did look adorable leaning on the doorway. "Did I upset you earlier?"

Alfie sort of nodded, but he really wasn't mad at Louis because sometimes people really did need a kick up the backside to realise what was good and wrong with their life.

"We're going to Sebastian's wedding," Alfie said going over and hugging Louis, "and then we can be happy,"

Louis kissed him. "I've always been happy and in love with you, but I just want you to be happy with yourself and your life,"

This whole everyone-knew-him-better-than-himself thing was seriously starting to annoy Alfie, but damn it, Alfie really loved it when Louis was all wise, adorable and just so bloody perfect.

But Alfie just knew the only reason why it annoyed him was because it was so true.

If he couldn't be happy with his life then the most important relationship in his life could never ever work out.

And that just terrified Alfie.

CHAPTER 6

The next morning Louis, beautiful Alfie and Penelope were all standing in Alfie's large office that Louis had actually missed, he had always like the idea of having an office. It was like having a permanent space of operations and somewhere that was actually his, instead of his constant, chaotic and deadly lifestyle of travelling around the UK and being loaned to international intelligence agencies as a mere pawn of the UK Government.

Louis really did love the stunning views of London, even in the rain, through Alfie's large floor-to-ceiling windows. London really did look impressive and innocent and seductive for a change instead of it being a city filled with deadly secrets that Louis had to expose and stop on a daily basis.

The sound of shuffling files and papers and mugs of strong bitter coffee that stunk out the office made Louis blow a kiss at his sexy stunning boyfriend as he sat down at his dark oak desk, and Penelope took a seat next to him.

Louis could never understand at all how Penelope could go on a late-night raid, fight a bunch of terrorists and kill them, all without looking tired or injured the next day. In fact she actually looked revitalised and even more beautiful than she normally did.

Penelope took a big file from the pile on Alfie's desk. "Let's get cracking then as I'm not on my honeymoon,"

Louis smiled and went over to the desk and grabbed another file as he sat down, savouring every minute with Alfie.

After doing so many missions apart, Louis had learnt to savour and treasure every single moment when him and Alfie were together, even if those moments were as unsexy as looking through Iranian intelligence reports from the MI5 lab with the results of the electronics that Penelope's dad had taken from the safehouse last night.

"I'm surprised to see you so great," Louis said.

Penelope shrugged. "You know what they say, there's no better medicine than killing scum in the night,"

Louis was fairly sure no one had ever said that in the history of MI5, 6 or the entire international intelligence community but she probably had a point.

Penelope slammed the file on the edge of the oak desk. "But mind you I'm having an awful problem with my phone company. I want them to repair my phone but they want a reason for the repair for *insurance* reasons,"

Louis just looked at Alfie and they both smiled at each other. This was very much a Pimple family reaction to a very simple problem, and it really spoke to the Pimple's position within MI5 that they didn't have to get their phones from MI5 directly like the rest of them did for national security reasons.

"I can't tell them that I was killing Iranians for King and country and the scumbag shot my phone. I'm terribly worried. I need my phone. What if there's a nuclear emergency and someone calls me?" Penelope asked.

Louis really wanted to be as nice as he could but that was going to be impossible so thankfully Alfie jumped in.

"You know," Alfie said, "you just say you dropped it on the floor and the screen smashed that way,"

"Oh you are perfect," Penelope shouted. "Simply perfect. I'll do that now,"

Louis was about to point to the intelligence file she was reading but Penelope had already fled the office before he could.

Alfie just laughed and it was such a cute little laugh, and Louis really liked seeing Alfie was in better spirits after last night. Louis still felt guilty about him saying their relationship was basically doomed because of him.

In a way it probably was unless Alfie really learnt

to deal with the betrayal that Sebastian caused and all the damage those newspaper reports had done, but Louis was going to fight for it no matter what.

"Still on for the wedding tonight?" Alfie asked.

Louis just smiled as he started reading a section on the list of top-Iranian commanders the attackers had been emailing in the hours before the Pimple estate was bombed.

"Hello?" Alfie asked.

Louis knew exactly what Alfie was trying to do, he really wanted Louis to be the one to turn round and forbid him from going to the wedding, and Alfie just wanted to chicken out, but that was the very, very last thing that Louis was going to allow him to do.

"I'll put it this way," Louis said. "We'll go to the wedding and you can undress me in my expensive wedding suit afterwards,"

Louis saw out of the corner of his eye Alfie pull down his file and fold his arms.

"I thought that happening anyway," Alfie said.

"It was but I'll only be wearing it if we go to the wedding,"

Alfie slowly nodded and picked up his file again.

As Louis read through more of the intelligence, including a very concerning email exchange between the head of the Iranian intelligence service and the now-dead Iranian terrorists about the UK's nuclear capabilities and how accurate their account was, Louis was just getting more and more worried for tomorrow.

Louis had known Alfie for two amazing years now and he knew sometimes Alfie could react in unsuspected ways. Like once Louis had bought Alfie a puppy because he had been saying how badly he missed his pet dog for his childhood, but Alfie was furious at Louis for getting him a puppy.

Because the reason his parents had had to get rid of the dog in the first place was that Alfie was severely allergic to them.

It still amazed Louis how quickly a nice gesture of love could end up in a hospital visit.

But for Alfie's sake Louis just really hoped tomorrow wasn't going to be a complete and utter disaster.

CHAPTER 7

Alfie's stomach twisted into a painful knot, his hands turned sweaty and his head felt dangerously light, and not at all in a good way, as he tightly gripped Louis's sexy strong hand and arm as they went into Sebastian's and Louie's wedding venue.

When it came to wedding venues, Alfie had always been of the firm opinion that the venue absolutely had to reflect the couple, otherwise it was all a little pointless. So considering Sebastian was a dark, twisted and horrific traitor and Louie looked like a 12 year old boy that looked rather stunning in makeup, Alfie was suspecting some kind of strange mixture of the two.

What he wasn't expecting was for the wedding to be inside an amazing castle that was owned by a Lord and Lady on their own country estate, Alfie had no idea Sebastian had friends at all let alone in high places.

The castle venue itself was a very long

rectangular shape with impressive grey stone almost growing out of the smooth polished white marble floor with immense old paintings, coats of arms and other historical artifacts lining the grey stone walls.

Alfie was surprised even the ceiling seemed to be decorative with golden lion heads roaring out from the ceiling with white diagonal titles all around them, and the entire place just looked stunning.

It was clear the Lord and Lady owners of the castle had money to burn, that was clear enough from the beautiful rose, apple and vegetable gardens outside. And all of this just made Alfie feel even worst about himself, he hadn't wanted to come here and now he was here it was just clear Sebastian did have everything in his perfect life, and Alfie only had sexy Louis in his.

Which wasn't all bad but he wanted more, he deserved more surely.

"MI6 or Counter-Terrorism," a very short little woman said as she gracefully walked up to Alfie wearing a little white dress.

Alfie wanted to speak but his throat dried up, Sebastian didn't deserve this at all.

"Counter-Terrorism," Louis said like it wasn't a complete lie.

The woman smiled and overdramatically pointed to the right hand side, Alfie managed a nod and then he just rested his shoulder on Louis's chest for a few moments.

After taking a few more steps forward, Alfie was

even more surprised by the amazing white marble benches they were using as seats. It was so much better than horrible ugly wooden pews from churches, the white marble benches were perfectly smooth and just flat out stunning to the eye.

Alfie really loved them and it almost felt like he was stepping inside a fairy tale. It just wasn't his fairy tale and the two people getting the fairy tale ending didn't deserve it.

Alfie let Louis guide them to the very end of the white marble bench at the very back of the wedding ceremony, which Alfie really appreciated at last he could bad mouth the wedding without how people seeing him.

All the other guests looked great and rather interesting with their massive hats, expensive designer dresses and suits, and Alfie was starting to feel rather undressed in his expensive black Italian suit.

"Are you okay?" Louis asked without his lips moving.

That ability of Louis was so cute and just amazing at times.

"Of course," Alfie said too quickly for it to be believable. "I am a master of my emotions and I'm interested to know how did a 12-year-old looking man who loves make up get high up into Counter-Terrorism. Yet another boys club in our profession,"

Louis laughed a little. "He's actually very good and he doesn't wear make-up at work and he's extremely straight acting at work too,"

Alfie just shook his head. He could never understand how people could keep their two lives so separate, because being gay or queer didn't make the person weird or whatever. It just made them normal and gay or queer, and Alfie couldn't understand why someone would want to keep their professional and gay part of themselves so separate.

But being a former (in all but name) intelligence officer himself, Alfie understood it. Unless you were a straight white man, the intelligence world was always against you.

"Where's-" Louis asked as he looked about.

Alfie instantly saw what he was looking at and the Pimples were here. Alfie had no clue that Sebastian had invited Penelope and her family, Penelope looked amazing in her bright ocean blue dress, curly blond hair and dark blue shoes.

Penelope quickly sat next to Alfie.

"Don't worry me and my family aren't really here. We're in disguise. There's a Pastini bomb threat on the wedding. Pretend I'm not here," she said.

Alfie just looked at Louis. "If we ever get married don't invite Penelope. She just brings trouble with her,"

Penelope playfully hit him. "I heard that and you're probably right.

A very tall elderly woman that was clearly from the British nobility stood up at the very front of the white marble benches wearing a very lovely large blue hat that thankfully covered up her face, an ocean blue dress and no shoes whatsoever. She had to be Sebastian's mother.

"And here comes the bride... I mean groom or whatever. I'm just here for... I don't know why I'm here. Maybe just the free alcohol I'm paying for,"

Alfie just smiled. Maybe Sebastian's mother was just as bad as her son and then wedding music from unknown speakers filled the castle hall and everyone stood up as Louie Carter entered the hall.

And Alfie seriously felt awful.

CHAPTER 8

As Louis stood up with the wedding music playing from unknown speakers, other wedding guests crying from the Counter-Terrorism side and guests moaning from the MI6 side, Louis just watched as Louie really did look beautiful.

Louis had to be the first to admit he wasn't the type of gay that wanted to do make-up have their nails painted and do all the stereotypical gay stuff. If other people wanted to do that then Louis was more than happy for them, maybe even a little jealous for them, but Louie really, really looked stunning.

Louis didn't remember Louie being so tall, but he looked great in his tall tight-fitting pink suit that really brought out the sapphire colour of his eyes, his nails were perfectly painted in baby pink and Louis completely agreed he did look so young and beautiful.

Louie's face was lightly and very tastefully covered in foundation that matched his skin tone perfectly (something so many people struggled with), his short black hair looked like it perfectly accented everything, and Louis really doubted he had seen a bigger smile than Louie as he walked down the aisle.

It was a bit sad that Louie was walking alone but to be honest if anyone else was with him, it really would detract from how amazing Louie looked on his wedding day.

"He's too beautiful. Sebastian doesn't deserve that," Alfie said almost silently.

Louis leant closer. "But remember you don't have to try to look that beautiful every day. You're more beautiful than Louie every day to me,"

Louis loved feeling Alfie quickly kiss the back of his head and he could have sworn he heard Alfie tearing up behind him.

After a few more moments, everyone sat back down again and the awful woman that was probably Sebastian's mother stood up again.

"Now the real star of the show. The love of my life, the apple of my eye and the bestest son I ever could have wished for, except a straight son,"

Louis's mouth just dropped as she said that. How dare she.

Then Louis quickly realised that surely the entire wedding had been done in the wrong order because surely the groom was meant to be standing up for the walking down the aisle.

Louis shrugged it off as everyone turned round to look as Sebastian walked down the aisle, but no one dared to stand up or smile or do much of anything really. It was only the people on the MI6 side that really seemed to do anything with a mere nod of their respect towards Sebastian.

Louis had to admit Sebastian was completely rubbish compared to his groom because all he was wearing was a black suit that was slightly shiny with some golden thread running through it. And Sebastian was walking so cockily that Louis just wanted to hit him.

Louis could literally feel the arrogance pour off Sebastian as he walked open and even dared to wink at Alfie.

"You could of had this if you weren't such a cry baby," Sebastian muttered as he walked past.

Louis just gripped Alfie's hand, and wanted, needed to love, protect and treasure him because this was clearly a mistake.

Louis had been so stupid for making Alfie come here, all Louis had wanted to do was make sure that Alfie was okay, realise that his life was perfect and that Sebastian hadn't destroyed him.

"I'm so sorry," Louis said.

Alfie shook Louis's hand free and folded his arms and leant over to Penelope. "Can you call in a bomb scare for little old me?"

Penelope looked like she was trying to keep a straight face but completely failed. "No,"

Louis wanted to kiss Alfie so badly but then Sebastian's mother stood up again and it became crystal clear that she was officiating the wedding.

Louis would never have allowed his mother to do it, simply because she was the complete opposite to Sebastian's.

And would be far too mushy for the wedding officiating to be coherent at all.

"I might not agree with this gay marriage crap," the mother said, "but I love my son and I love his... special friend,"

Louis just looked at Alfie and at least he was smiling because they really weren't going to need to be thinking about their wedding jokes. The comments about the wedding were writing themselves.

"Sebastian my son, you may do your vows,"

Alfie sat up perfectly straight, Louis tried to grab his hand away but Alfie shook it away each time.

"Beautiful Louie. When I first met you, I was a mess, I was just out from a bad relationship where I had stupidly sold my boyfriend's secrets and those of our great nation to the press for a mere few million,"

Louis gasped that Sebastian had actually included that of all things in his wedding vows.

"But when I met you, you taught me how to love, forgive and think of others again, and unlike my last boyfriend you taught me how to be normal and actually have fun,"

Louis really tried not to smile for Alfie's sake but it was just so outrageous Sebastian was using his wedding vows as a weapon against Alfie. That was so low of him.

"And as I marry you today, no matter what

happens be it sickness, health or bad times, I will always be by your side because unlike my last boyfriend you love me, support me and treasure me no matter what. That is exactly what love should be like,"

"Ah that's nice," Sebastian's mother said.

Louis quickly looked at Alfie and he was just sitting there perfectly straight and expressionless. In all the time Louis had known Alfie that meant only one thing.

He was outraged. And rightfully so.

"My son's special friend Louie now you can say your vows," Sebastian's mother said.

It only dawned on Louis the sheer age gap between Sebastian and Louie, with Louie being easily ten or twelve years younger than his soon-to-be husband, not that it mattered. It was just a bit of a surprise.

"Beautiful," Louie said very high-pitched.

As Louie continued his very nice and flowery vows, Louis just smiled at them. Not because he agreed with how angelic and divine and special Louie made Sebastian sound but because of how happy he looked.

Louis really liked that Louie was happy and that he was acting like himself, his true self, on his wedding day. He didn't have to fake who he was, the fact that he liked makeup or anything on this special day.

Louie was just being himself and Louis really

loved that.

A few minutes later Sebastian's god awful mother announced they were married and Louis's stomach flipped and sank inside him.

Now they were going to the reception and the sit down.

Louis just hoped Alfie could contain his rage long enough not to make a scene at the reception. No matter how justified it would have been.

If Alfie made a scene in front of this guest list Louis seriously doubted he or even the Pimples could get Alfie out of that mess.

CHAPTER 9

After a great few hours of amazing food, very good music and a couple sensational dances with stunning Louis, Alfie sat at a very high bar stool next to a round wooden bar that formed an island in amongst the buffet on one side and the massive dance floor on the other, next to Penelope who looked as if she was about to fall off the stool and fall to her death at any moment.

Alfie had rather liked the past few hours, and he had had so much non-alcoholic cocktails that he was starting to think he would never have to drink again with their being so many amazing choices these days, and it seemed like all the alcoholic drinks had a non-alcoholic equal which Louis had already enjoyed a lot of, but at least Alfie was starting to warm up to the idea of non-alcoholic drinks.

Surely that was a great sign of development?

And it wasn't a sign whatsoever that Alfie was just as lame as when he had met Sebastian and been as boring and awful as he said in his own bloody wedding vows.

Alfie couldn't believe that Sebastian had done something that outrageous. How dare Sebastian do that, Alfie just hated him after everything he had done to him.

"You feeling okay?" Penelope asked. "You've been sulking for an hour and my bank account is running a little too empty to keep buying drinks whilst I wait for you,"

"Haven't you got bombers to search the grounds for?" Alfie asked.

Penelope shrugged. "What bombers?"

Alfie straightened his back. "You know the reason why you said you were here,"

"We lied," Penelope shouted over the loud techno music they were playing now. "We were annoyed we weren't invited so we crashed it,"

Alfie wished he had a drink at that moment so he could cheer her, sometimes even the Pimple's sheer uncaring attitude towards the rules surprised him.

"Al!" Sebastian shouted from across the buffet side of the reception area.

Alfie felt his stomach flip and pain flooded him like someone had just punched him in the stomach.

Alfie still couldn't see Louis and hadn't for ages. The last time Alfie had seen him was when Louis and another young man from GCHQ, the British NSA, were discussing how best to interrogate a Russian agent. Alfie still had no clue why someone from

GCHQ would want to know that.

Sebastian came over and hugged Alfie and kissed him lightly on the cheek, and Alfie seriously just wanted to throw Sebastian's plate of fish, chips and sauces all over his expensive looking suit.

"How dare you use your wedding vows as a weapon against me," Alfie said, forcing himself to remain calm.

"That was crappy of you," Penelope said.

Sebastian shrugged. "Only joking and you saw how great my husband is. If life was a game I clearly won and you clearly lost,"

Alfie couldn't understand why Sebastian was being like this. All Alfie had ever been to him was nice, loving and faithful, and even when all newspapers and news stations wanted to interview *the idiot gay spy* after Sebastian had sold him out, Alfie had denied them all.

All out of some stupid idea that Sebastian was still a good guy and had done what he did for a good reason.

"What has Alfie done to you?" Penelope asked.

Sebastian just smiled as his husband came over and kissed him. Alfie hated seeing Louie so in loved and caring towards the snake.

Alfie just wanted Louie to run and hide but legally speaking Alfie was fairly sure that was a useless option now, and they probably shared everything legally, including all of Louie's money.

Sebastian grinned at Alfie. "I don't know. It isn't

what you actually did, it's about what job you could have gotten,"

Alfie was just shocked and everything about the last few years became crystal clear and even the rumours had to be true.

At the time of the newspaper reports coming out, Alfie had heard plenty of rumours about him being transferred to MI6 to head up a brand new taskforce with a big budget, high stake missions and plenty of attention from the top of the agency.

If Alfie had done well then that taskforce could have made his career as every agency and everyone from the CIA to French DGSE and even the UK's secret secret-service (another much smaller division of MI6) wanting him to be *their* agent.

It could have changed his life for the better.

"You stole my career?" Alfie asked.

Then Alfie noticed that Louis was standing right behind Sebastian looking furious.

Sebastian laughed, nodded at Louis and started to walk away.

"We'll never know and you'll never have your career back loser," Sebastian said.

Louis looked like he was about to grab Sebastian but Alfie threw himself off the very high barstool and "accidentally" landed on Louis so he couldn't do anything else.

Alfie started kissing him to make sure Louis didn't push him and start following Sebastian at his own wedding. But at least he now knew the truth about why Sebastian had sold him out all those years ago.

It wasn't national security, a good reason or even money, it was all about making sure Sebastian could have a great career instead of Alfie, and that just fucked him off more than anything else in the entire world.

And Alfie just had to make Sebastian pay for that.

CHAPTER 10

Two days later, Louis was extremely glad his killer hangover had finally worn off as he sat on one of the two chairs in Alfie's great office, but the bright light coming in from the massive floor-to-ceiling windows were a little off putting and it was wait to bright for a morning.

Granted the views of skyscrapers, traffic and an ever-growing stream of people walking on the streets below them were stunning, Louis just wasn't sure if his minorly pounding head could handle such light this early in the morning, despite it being nine o'clock.

Louis didn't know why he had gotten so mad, angry and outraged when Sebastian finally confessed to why he sold out Alfie all those years ago, but he just had to keep drinking the whiskey to stop him from knocking Sebastian's lights out, and now he really understood why Alfie was so silent.

Louis just looked at the beautiful, stunning love of his life as he sat there emailing the results of the intelligence reports he had discovered, analysed and read. He was speed typing and pounding his pretty little fingers into the keyboard so he was annoyed but silent.

Louis heard high heels behind him and he was a little unsure why Penelope was coming to see them when she had texted yesterday saying she was meant to be looking at the new "highly secured" wedding venue.

Penelope put her hand on her hips in her light blue dress like she was waiting for Alfie to talk to her. Louis himself had been sitting here for an hour flicking through her reports and Alfie hadn't spoken to him once.

"You'll be waiting an hour. He's sulking," Louis said.

"I'm not fucking sulking. I'm annoyed that my dickhead of an ex is having my career whilst I'm stuck emailing stupid agents without a single thank you," Alfie said.

"Can you email me those reports on North Korea agents in Liverpool later please?" Louis said smiling.

Alfie didn't even smile that he had accidentally forgotten his own boyfriend was in his to-email-list.

"Louie Carter is here to see you," Penelope said.

Alfie stopped typing and frowned. If looks could kill, Louis was certain him and Penelope would be dead by now.

"Just him?" Alfie asked.

"Yes and here he is," Penelope said, rushing to the door and gesturing him in.

Louis was about to leave when Penelope came in after Louie and close the large glass door behind them all. Clearly Louis wasn't the only one who secretly wanted to watch this.

Louis and Penelope both folded their arms and leant closer like they were watching a great movie and thankfully that managed to make Alfie smile a little.

Louie seemed a little put off as he stood there in his blue suit, youthful face covered in excellent make-up and his baby pink nails.

"What do you want?" Alfie asked.

"Thank you for coming," Louie said high pitched. "It meant a lot I mean,"

Louis actually thought that Sebastian was lying when he told Alfie it was a condition of their marriage but it was even stranger that it turned out to be true.

"When I found out what he did to you I broke up with him. I hated him and was sure it would happen to me,"

"It still could," Louis said quietly. Alfie smiled and Penelope hit Louis round the ear.

Louie didn't seem to notice. "I just wanted to, you know, see if you were okay. I didn't want to marry him if I saw you were a wreck and he had destroyed your life,"

"Why marry him then?" Penelope asked.

It was a good question but Louis still didn't want to say anything in case he was "interfering" with a "private" conversation.

Louie smiled like such a schoolboy. "Because sometimes you need to roll the dice on love,"

Louis was fairly sure Alfie was going to start shouting or protesting that Louie had it completely wrong but all Alfie did was smile, not a fake one but a real one.

"I'm alive and I'm well and as an intelligence officer that's all that matters," Alfie said.

Louie cocked his head and his voice changed to a lower pitch. "You're only well. Haven't you heard what's happening in Counter-Terrorism?"

Louis loved it how everyone leant closer as one.

"What?" Penelope asked.

Louie smiled. "The head of the agency has been fired for sexual harassment and racism. I'm unofficially on the shortlist to be the new head and I know of another agent on the shortlist for one of the new department heads,"

"Really him?" Louis asked, sounding way too surprised for it not to be insulting.

Alfie kicked Louis under the desk. "You mean I could be a head of department for counter-terrorism?"

"It would be a step up from your analyst position," Louie said. "You know UK threats like no one else, your intelligence has stopped more terror threats than anyone else and you're a very capable agent,"

Louis really smiled. This was amazing news and

now he just needed to work out how to make sure Alfie got it.

"But I will confess Sebastian has applied on the same head and is on the same shortlist as you, and whilst I would personally not recommend him for any position within my organisation, the personnel choice of the department is question is not within my powers if you catch my drift,"

Louis just coughed as he realised there was only one department within Counter-Terrorism that was organised more by the government with the consultation of head of Counter-Terrorism than anything else. Alfie was being shortlisted to head the Political and Global Affairs division, that was one of the most important divisions in the country.

Whoever controlled that division of Counter-Terrorism had to work with all the foreign intelligence agencies, MI5 and MI6 to protect not only UK politicians but terrorism and assassination plots against heads of state and other politicians on UK soil.

It was sort of a department with the responsibilities of MI5 and MI6 merged together.

Whoever ruled the department was extremely powerful in the UK intelligence community, and the international one for that matter.

"Thank you," Alfie said as he clearly realised what that meant judging from his face.

"My pleasure but Sebastian's influence is growing so be careful," Louie said as he left and nodded his respects to Louis and Penelope.

As Louis saw Penelope rush over to Alfie, hug and laugh with him about how amazing the news was Louis just felt a little sick.

As he also knew that if Sebastian got one of the most powerful jobs in all UK intelligence work then he just knew it would destroy Alfie.

And Louis seriously doubted Sebastian wasn't going to use his position to get Alfie kicked out of the intelligence community for good.

Louis really couldn't allow that to happen. He just didn't know how to stop it.

CHAPTER 11

Alfie absolutely couldn't believe it was eleven o'clock at night as he went down the long narrow grey corridor with breath-taking views of London's immense skyline, bright lights on top of other penthouses and banking buildings and there was even a plane or two in the sky to his left from the large glass windows, as he went towards his and Louis's penthouse apartment.

The corridor didn't have many doors or paintings or anything really, to give the walls any texture or personality but Alfie just supposed that was by design, and forced people to look at the stunning views outside.

Alfie completely couldn't remember the last time he had been home this late before, maybe when he first started work at MI5, but definitely not for years. He was normally finished at 5 pm and back home for 6. He wasn't the so-called good agent that worked overtime for no reason.

But ever since Louie had told him about being short-listed, Alfie had wanted to work harder, smarter and really show that he was the best man for the job. So Alfie had completely emptied his intelligence report pile, send tons of different agents emails about new assassination targets, and Alfie had even managed to locate a terrorist in Cardiff, Wales that MI5 had wanted for twenty years.

Alfie really wanted this job.

As Alfie kept walking down the narrow corridor towards his penthouse apartment, he was really looking forward to seeing beautiful, sexy Louis again, and hearing about his day and now just being a real person and a boyfriend, instead of the Super-Agent mask that he had effectively put on today.

Alfie reached his and Louis's black wooden door, opened it and was surprised by the smell of freshly baked chocolate cake, burnt something and Louis's aftershave in the air. It wasn't a special occasion or something (Alfie really hoped it wasn't), so he went down into the living room and just smiled.

He loved it how Louis was laying on their large black sofa completely asleep and quietly snoring away, with a range of orange-scented candles burnt down to the bottom on the coffee table, and now the entire coffee table was covered in melted wax.

But Alfie really loved how Louis had presumably baked him a chocolate cake, his favourite, and put now melted candles on it. It was a shame that the top of the chocolate cake was now ruined as was the thick velvety double chocolate icing.

Yet it was the thought that counted.

An intense wave of emotion washed over Alfie and he couldn't believe that Louis had done something for him. It couldn't have been easy with Louis finishing work at 5 pm after a busy day of meetings with different intelligence agents and travelling to the South West for a quick mission and getting back to London for 5.

But Louis had still managed to buy the ingredients, make it and try to make something simply magical for him, not anyone else, just Alfie.

And that really, really made him feel very special.

Alfie carefully went over to the black sofa making sure not to disturb the love of his life and sat down, and he couldn't help but think of what Louie had said earlier, about everyone needs to role the dice on love.

There were a lot of weddings going on at the moment and Alfie had actually loved helping Penelope with hers, it had been fun going to Sebastian's minus the crap about the wedding vows but it had been fun. And Louis had been there for Alfie since the beginning and without him Alfie actually had no idea if he would still be an agent or even alive for that matter.

He really did owe and love and treasure Louis for everything.

Alfie just knew that he had to ask Louis to marry him, because of course he still had a lot of problems and difficulties to get through because of his past with Sebastian and that betrayal, but Alfie really, really didn't want to overcome these problems without Louis by his side.

Because he loved him.

Alfie got down on one knee with the cold wooden floorboards sending nervous chills up into his body and Alfie gently tapped Louis's knee.

Louis shot up, whipping out a gun and scanned the room.

"It's me," Alfie said, not sure to be impressed or not but he smiled anyway because Louis was always so, so cute when he had just woken up.

Louis looked a little embarrassed and then looked really sad as he looked at the coffee table and cake covered in melted wax.

"Sorry I'm home so late," Alfie said. "It looks beautiful,"

Louis grinned. "I was hoping you would get to see it in person,"

Alfie's smile only grew and his stomach filled with butterflies as he realised that he was about to ask a question that could completely change his life for the better or worst through sickness and health.

"Louis O'Deal will you marry me?"

CHAPTER 12

Louis wasn't completely sure if he was dreaming or something but he absolutely couldn't believe what he was hearing. It sounded as if his beautiful stunning Alfie had literally just asked him to marry him.

Louis felt his entire body turn sweaty, his entire head went light and he just seriously thought he was about to faint. This couldn't be happening, he had wanted this moment for so long but he had never ever expected sexy Alfie to be the one to propose.

Louis was about to open his mouth when Alfie's phone rang. The ringtone broke the tense silence that Louis hadn't realised had fallen across their penthouse living room with the people in their paintings seemingly watching Louis too.

The phone kept ringing.

"Of course I'll marry you!" Louis shouted.

Louis fell forward landing and almost tackling Alfie to the ground as the two newly engaged lovers started kissing, hugging and preparing for a great night of sex.

The phone kept ringing.

Louis really didn't care what the phone call was about. He only wanted to focus on the amazing feeling of Alfie's skinny firm body under him and his soft tasty lips against his.

Louis's phone started ringing.

Alfie pushed Louis away, and Louis was almost disappointed until he looked at his phone screen and realised that it was Penelope calling him, and Penelope's mother was calling Alfie.

They both just looked at each other and if the Pimples were calling both of them then something very wrong was happening and Louis just knew that their nice calm evening of celebrating their engagement, talking about the wedding and having a lot of great celebratory sex was over.

Their plans were as dead as the man Louis had killed earlier for King and Country.

Louis answered it and put it on speaker so his sexy new fiancée could listen in.

"Agent O'Deal and Steward here you're on speaker," Louis said to Penelope.

"Mummy I got them both," Penelope said sounding terribly upset.

"What's wrong?" Alfie asked.

"My daddy. He's... he's been shot in the chest three times. He was out shooting with some friends but his best friend betrayed him and shot at him," Penelope said.

Louis heard the phone exchange hands.

"My husband," Penelope's mum said through crying and tears, "is... not going to make it. He's, dying and Penny. Just get here now!"

The phone link went dead and Louis just couldn't believe what had happened. Penelope's father was a legend in the intelligence community, a true hero of the UK that actually loved all the Scottish, English and Welsh with even some respect for the Northern Irish people. That respect for all four nations was something so few members of the UK elite had these days.

And Penelope's father was just an amazing man and knew he was dying.

Louis's phone buzzed with the address of the hospital and Louis just looked at Alfie with his beautiful wet eyes, vulnerable look and he really did look so beautiful and Louis really couldn't imagine his life without them.

Louis kissed him hard on the lips, just savouring their softness and taste in case what happened to Penelope's father ever happened to him.

"We better get going," Alfie said sounding both disappointed and sad about the death and how the Pimples had basically ruined their engagement.

But Louis just grabbed Alfie's hand as he tried to stand up and pulled Alfie onto Louis, kissing him again.

"I do love you and I really want to marry you. You're amazing, smart and funny, and I mean it when

I say, my life is nothing without you," Louis said.

Alfie bit his lip and nodded. Louis knew it was probably what Alfie had always wanted to hear from someone he loved, instead of them selling him out to the newspapers and media.

"Now let's go and help our friend," Louis said rubbing Alfie's leg before they both got up and headed straight out the door.

But as much as Louis didn't want to think about Penelope's father dying. He had to admit it did give them an even better opportunity to get one over on Sebastian because now the Deputy Director of MI5 was vacant and that position was slightly better than the department head opportunity at Counterterrorism.

There were a lot of moving parts and Louis just hoped Alfie didn't get hurt going after the opportunities he so rightfully deserved.

CHAPTER 13

Alfie didn't know how but it was just flat out typical that something like this would happen when he had literally just proposed to the love of his life, and as soon as beautiful Louis had said yes the entire world seemed to be falling apart.

It was seriously impossible that a legend like Penelope's father had simply been shot by his best friend, something else had to be going on, and Alfie just wasn't impressed.

As him and his sexy new fiancée went down a sterile white wide hospital corridor with tons of wooden doors shooting off into large hospital rooms in a top-secret location, Alfie just felt sick. Granted that could have been because of the sheer amount of lemony cleaning chemicals that the hospitals seemed to use by the bucket full but Alfie still wasn't impressed.

The sound of nurses and patients and doctors shouting about gods knows what filled the corridor, and Alfie kept a look out for Penelope and her mum. All Alfie wanted to do in that moment (besides from celebrate his own engagement properly) was hug Penelope.

She was definitely going to need it.

A few moments later a very tall woman with long blond hair, blue high-heels and a light blue dress walked out of one of the rooms and Alfie waved at her.

Thankfully it was Penelope or Alfie just would have died inside out of embarrassment if he had been waving at a random woman.

Alfie and Louis both quickened their pace down to her and Alfie hugged Penelope. It was clear from her ruined make-up that she had been crying a lot and as Penelope led them into the sterile white hospital room with her father in a large blue hospital bed with ridiculous thin sheets, she started crying again.

Alfie gasped and covered his mouth as he watched Penelope's father, a very muscular man in his fifties with no facial hair or injuries and still a full head of brown hair, just laid there dying.

Alfie gripped Louis's strong arms even more and they slowly went towards the hospital bed. Penelope closed the wooden door to their room and tapped her father on the shoulder.

"Are we good?" her father asked, his voice rough like sandpaper.

"Yes," Penelope said.

Alfie didn't understand what was going on in the

slightest but he knew that if the Pimples were up to something they were about to tell them what was going on, so Alfie just folded his arms.

Penelope's father pushed himself up, stretched and smiled at Alfie and Louis. "Thanks for coming so soon guys. I tell you it was a real pain in the ass to get shot by your best friend. I'm even going to have to stay here for a few days recovering. Thank God for your intelligence Alfie,"

Alfie's eyes widened he had filed and read so many intelligence reports today he actually didn't know what her father was talking about.

"Explain please?" Louis asked.

"Your boyfriend here is sensational. He found a link between Iranian money coming into the UK, a bank that my best friend was an investor in and I managed to use that connection to work out he was an Iranian agent," her father said.

"You're welcome sir," Alfie said not knowing what else to do.

Her father came over and hugged Alfie. "Don't be silly, call me Alfred,"

"Okay... Alfred," Alfie said nervously. He had just been hugged by the deputy director of MI5, that was a big deal.

Louis clicked his fingers. "Wait. Iranians bombed your country estate. Iranians attacked you in the raid. And now the Iranians tried to assassinate you. What's really going on?"

That was a great question and Alfie really wished

he had asked it.

Alfred looked at his wife and daughter. "When the US pulled out the Iran Nuclear Deal it sent shockwaves through the world and the middle east that the US was weak, and the western world was leaderless,"

Alfie nodded, he might have been MI5 and focused on the UK domestically, but he had still seen those scary reports.

Penelope stepped forward. "So the Iranians started up their nuclear programme much faster than any of us ever thought possible without the help of even China or Russia,"

Alfie gasped. He didn't even know how that was possible and the sheer political consequences of Iran having nuclear weapons would change the middle-east forever, and not in a good way.

"Thankfully," Alfred's wife said, "me and a couple of other agents in MI5 and 6 decided to take action first with a few operations that twisted the rules of our agencies,"

"And we kidnapped and killed Iran's top nuclear scientist," Penelope said.

Alfie nodded as he finally understood it all. "And now they want revenge against the Pimple family,"

Everyone else just nodded.

"But for these sort of events to happen there would have to be a cell working within the UK and a leader of the Iran cell is unknown," Alfred said.

Alfie suddenly realised why him and Louis had

been invited. "You want me and Louis to work with your wife and Penelope, don't you? To find out what happened and who's behind it,"

Alfred nodded and hugged Alfie again, hugging one of his bosses just felt weird.

"And if you find it out for me," Alfred said, "I will personally make the government assign you as head of Political and Global Affairs of Counterterrorism and I will reveal everything I have on Sebastian Crawford. His career would be over and he would finally be vulnerable enough to be charged with treason,"

Those words slammed into Alfie like icy cold hammer blows at the idea Alfred had blackmail material on Sebastian that wouldn't only destroy him, but finally allow Alfie to have a career again.

Alfie just looked at his beautiful fiancée and he really loved it how excited Louis looked.

"We're in," Louis said.

Alfie felt so excited but he had to admit he was a little nervous about going after the Iranians. They had always bombed and killed people.

And Alfie absolutely couldn't allow that to happen to the man he loved. No matter what Alfie had to do to stop it.

CHAPTER 14

The next morning Louis went into Alfie's large spacious office with its floor-to-ceiling windows with stunning views of the London skyline, Alfie's dark oak desk and two blue fabric chairs in front of it. But he was a lot more interested in the heavy aroma of bitter black coffee that basically stunk out the entire office.

Louis had known he had had to force Alfie to go to bed last night, because all he had really wanted to do last night was start working on the Iranian case, rather obsessively, and Alfie had left home at 7 am this morning, but Louis hadn't realised he had been working for a while.

It was only 9 am and normally Louis and Alfie walked into work together but clearly Alfie just wanted to focus on the Iranian case, yet he wasn't in his office yet.

"Where's our favourite gay superspy?" Penelope asked as she came up behind Louis.

Louis glanced at her and was slightly annoyed that even after all the drama of last night with her father "dying" (a lie they all still had to keep telling) Penelope still looked as fresh and beautiful and stunning as she always did.

Louis was starting to wonder what actually made her look bad. "Dunno and aren't you meant to be readjusting your wedding dress or doing wedding-y things?"

Penelope nodded. "Maybe later," then she started fake crying very well. "I'm just so upset for my daddy,"

Louis forced himself not to laugh as Penelope cried into his shoulder as he noticed three cleaners walk past and nod their respects to Penelope.

"They're gone," Louis said.

"Thank god I didn't think I could keep me-self going any longer," Penelope said.

The sound of something bashing metal and glass made Louis look at beautiful Alfie as he stumbled out of the metal lift holding a rather destroyed bouquet of pink roses with a couple white lilies added.

Louis wasn't even going to mention why the white lilies were slightly inappropriate.

"What happened to you?" Louis asked giving Alfie a quick kiss.

"It was a nightmare. I was working at my desk for an hour on the Iranian case when I realised I couldn't make it look like Alfred was dead if I hadn't got Penelope some flowers,"

Louis nodded, made sense and now he felt bad.

"Then I was running out to the corner shop with the florist next door," Alfie said. "Got the flowers but then a massive pitbull looked at me and started chasing me into the building,"

Louis bit his lip.

"Then!" Alfie said. "The stupid building security let the pit bull inside thinking it was my pet. The dog chased me into the lift where I had to fight it off with the flowers until the lift doors opened on the first floor and I kicked it out, without hurting it of course,"

Louis just nodded. Wow.

"Why was it chasing you?" Penelope asked.

Alfie looked to the ground and focused on his shoes. "It was in heat,"

Louis just laughed. That was brilliant.

Alfie passed the half-beaten flowers to Penelope and she pretended to get emotional and very teary. Louis hadn't realised she was such a great actress.

Alfie pushed past them both and went into his office, and as Louis followed he had a good look at his fiancée's amazing ass on the way.

Penelope closed the large glass door behind them. "What did you find?"

Louis took a seat on the blue fabric chair and looked at Alfie.

"Your investigation was very good," Alfie said, "not that I expected anything less from the Pimples but you were right. The Iranian embassy did swarm the safehouse after your raid and even the Ambassador to the UK turned up,"

Louis cocked his head a little. That was a little odd considering Ambassadors mainly just stayed at the Embassy in London and didn't really travel much unless it was an event.

"Why did he go?" Louis asked Penelope.

"We don't know but I watched for a little bit until a guard found out and I snapped her neck," Penelope said. "The Ambassador only seemed to be getting a report,"

Louis nodded. It made sense, the chances of the Ambassador being the ring leader of the Iranian cell was microscopic because most foreign powers preferred to keep their diplomats in the dark about such illegal operations just in case they were ever asked about them, and plausibility, deniability and all that.

"But this cell we're investigating," Louis said, "we know it's the same cell from your report but who are the members?"

Alfie waved his hand excitedly at Louis. "From the sieged electronics from the raid, I managed to find five contacts not including the leader, and because of the Pimples' investigation we now know three of their names,"

Louis nodded as Alfie turned round his computer screen and showed him and Penelope three very muscular and deadly looking Iranian spies. He had seen them a few times on different Wanted Lists and in intelligence reports on certain bombings, and they always operated with the same people.

It just wasn't until now anyone knew they were connected to each other.

"Where are they now?" Penelope asked.

If she was thinking of paying them a visit then Louis was really going to like working with Penelope.

"In London for an Iranian cultural event at a small Middle Eastern museum maybe ten minutes away," Alfie said.

Penelope nodded and looked at them both. "You want to join me for some cultural enlightenment?"

Louis stretched his arm over to Alfie's and Alfie took it. "We will but there's something we need to tell you first. If you're okay with that Alfie?"

Alfie just laughed and Louis almost felt bad for basically forcing him to tell Penelope about their engagement.

But thankfully Alfie just looked like the cutest schoolboy with his little grin in happiness than Louis had ever seen.

CHAPTER 15

Alfie was so relieved when Penelope screamed in delight and hugged and kissed him and Louis when he told her they were engaged. Alfie hadn't really expected any other sort of reaction but to actually see it, it was such a great feeling. And it only made Alfie love Penelope and sexy Louis even more.

It was hardly a big surprise when he, Louis and Penelope got to the little Middle Eastern Museum in their formal MI5 wear that everyone there acted with suspicion and immediately closed ranks. It was only made worse when Penelope, in typical Pimple style, demanded to speak with the three suspects they had come to see on suspicion of terrorism against the UK.

Even now as Alfie, the love of his life and Penelope stood in a little white box room with a wooden bench in the middle, bright cream-coloured walls and ancient paintings from the 16th century of middle eastern coffee houses hanging on the walls, still didn't understand why Penelope had revealed why they wanted to see the three men.

Thankfully Alfie normally loved the Middle Eastern none of them were bad people per se in the slightest. It was only their hard-line politicians and extremely anti-western views that were the problem, but most of the time the Middle Eastern people were some of the most interesting Alfie had ever had the pleasure of knowing.

"Salaam," a middle-aged Iranian man said placing his hand over his heart and bowing his head slightly towards Penelope.

Alfie instantly recognised him as Ali Javadi, one of the three terrorists they were meant to meet but Alfie couldn't see the other two for now.

"Salaam," the three of them said back as a sign of respect.

Alfie wasn't sure why they were being so respectful but he was going to let Penelope take the lead here, and in all fairness at least Ali was trying to be kind. It might actually make things easier for all of them.

Ali came and stood next to Alfie as they looked at an old painting of a coffee house.

"What do you really know of this?" Ali asked. Alfie was surprised it was a real question without a hint of disrespect.

Alfie smiled. "Coffee drinking is hardly new in Iran because it can easily be traced back to the 16th century with the Safavid dynasty with coffee houses, or Qahve Khaneh, sorry about my pronunciation were a gathering place for artists and poets,"

Ali nodded and laughed a little. "You know stuff,"

Louis came to stand on the other side of Ali. "And the term *house* in Iran unlike in other cultures can be used to refer to a café without coffee needing to be served,"

Ali nodded and clapped his hands. "At least I now know that MI5 agents that kill and murder my people in cold blood understand our culture a little,"

Alfie was surprised that he actually felt respect towards Ali for saying that, he wasn't being a slimy diplomat or trying to be one when he wasn't. He was just speaking his mind and there was something very respectable in that.

"We know you did bombings in Paris, Madrid and Chicago," Penelope said. "You're on MI5's Wanted List for extradition to whatever country we want to send you first but I will not arrest you this time if you tell us what we need to know,"

Ali laughed. "My country wouldn't allow you to arrest me anyway so your threats are meaningless. And my two countrymen, is that how say it in English, are safe away,"

Alfie just shook his head, maybe this slim ball was as slimy as he feared in the first place.

"Who's your handler?" Alfie asked.

Another five much older Iranian men walked in and Alfie carefully took a photo of them with his smartphone as he pretended to take a photo of the painting.

"Leave," one of the five men said.

Alfie, Penelope and Louis respectfully bowed their heads slightly and left.

Alfie just hoped the photo would reveal something but it was becoming deadly clear now that the leader had to be someone very high up in the Iranian hierarchy.

And that really concerned Alfie especially with Penelope's wedding in two days.

CHAPTER 16

Louis was seriously hoping Alfie's amazingly clever photo would finally reveal something and give them a real solid lead as they sat around Alfie's dark oak wooden desk in his beautiful office. Louis was really glad the strong bitter coffee smell was gone now, and replaced with something a lot sweeter, almost caramelly from Penelope's spiced tea she had bought on the way back from the little museum.

"Just a few more moments," Alfie said.

Louis loved watching sexy Alfie's fingers race over his keyboard as he tried to match the faces of the five much older men with known terrorists and intelligence players in Iran. Alfie just looked so cute and adorable and intelligent as he worked, and Louis was so excited about getting to marry this stunning man.

Even since he was a little twelve-year-old boy, when Louis had first realised he was gay, he had wanted to find a beautiful man, find love and get married. He had never planned out his ideal fantasy wedding but Louis grew up in a small English town that didn't support gay marriage in the slightest, so now he was actually getting married he was completely overjoyed, excited and even a little nervous.

Marriage was for life and it was special, Louis really didn't want to mess it up for Alfie, and he seriously wanted the entire day to be perfect for them both, but more for Alfie after everything he had had to deal with.

"Done," Alfie said smiling.

Louis and Penelope leant closer as Alfie bought up the facial IDs of one of the much-older men from the photo whilst the computer software continued to run the four other men through their databases.

"We are looking at Amir-Coffeian from Iranian Intelligence and brother to the two other men we wanted to talk too at the museum but Ali didn't allow us," Alfie said.

"What do we have on him?" Penelope asked.

Louis looked at both of them. "When I was on loan to the French DGSE last week, there was a large taskforce dedicated to hunting this guy down after they bombed the French embassy in Iran killing twenty women and ten men,"

Penelope just shook her head, Louis completely agreed with how outrageous Amir was.

Alfie's beautiful fingers danced over his keyboard a little more. "And MI5 was monitoring him for a time as soon as he landed but he has never committed a crime on UK soil and we've never seen reason to arrest him before,"

"I think the French could give us a good reason," Louis said.

Penelope cocked her head a little. "I could contact the Government for permission to arrest Amir, interrogate him on why he's hanging around with Ali before handing them over to the French,"

Louis laughed. "That's cute you think the Government would want to hand over a prisoner to the French for free,"

Penelope nodded and stood up. "It's worth a try,"

Louis shrugged because it was a pointless try because Ali had been right in the museum, even if Iran did allow their agents to be arrested and charged by MI5, Louis just couldn't see the UK Government wanting to keep Iranians in jail considering the rumours about a UK-Iran deal for oil being in the works.

And that would only make it harder to interrogate and find out what they were working on.

"You okay?" Alfie asked looking away from his computer.

Louis grinned at Alfie, he really was so beautiful. "Yea just hoping we can solve this case,"

"Agreed," Alfie said. "If facial recognition brings up nothing we need to go back to basics and relook over everything the Pimples investigated up to the shooting. Including how the hell they bombed the Pimple country estate,"

Louis was almost surprised he hadn't thought of that before, granted both Louis and Alfie had thought it was simply because the Pimples had kept such poor security on their estate with the wedding coming up, but in reality that wasn't like them.

In fact Louis would have been surprised if there wasn't a four-digit number spent on security for before the wedding alone, it was no myth that Alfred was overprotective of his only daughter when she wasn't doing intelligence work, so how did the bomb and Iranians get into the estate in the first place?

"Good point," Louis said then he took Alfie's hand in his and kissed it. "How about tonight we go out for dinner and plan *our* wedding?"

Alfie gave Louis such a cute schoolboy grin but the moment was ruined when Alfie's computer bleeped.

"Nothing," he said. "Our databases have no clue who the men are and I ever expanded the search to other middle-eastern countries. These men are either unknown to the Intelligence community or they're British born,"

That wasn't good in the slightest. Louis had seriously wanted a new lead so it looked like him and Alfie were going to have to travel up North to see the Pimple family estate.

And for some reason Louis just knew he was going to very much regret it.

CHAPTER 17

It was hardly surprising when the Home Secretary of the UK wrote back to Penelope and gave an extremely firm no on arresting Amir and giving him over to the disgusting Frogs (the French to normal people) but Alfie was hardly surprised and at least it meant that now Penelope could join him and Louis as they travelled to her country estate.

Alfie had only ever been the country estate in Yorkshire for a couple of times because it was one of the most exclusive estates in the country, and the Pimples rarely used themselves, and instead liked to rent it out to politicians and other people who the Pimples wanted favours from, and Alfie was rather surprised to know it actually worked.

"Here we are everyone. Home sweet home," Penelope said from the backseat.

As Louis pulled their black Land Rover gently to a stop on the little multicoloured gravel of the driveway, Alfie was just shocked at the sheer amazing look at the country manor with its immensely tall stone brick walls that went up three stories with large Victorian windows facing outwards. Alfie really loved the little red front door and the polished marble steps that were so close to them.

And a very tall female butler had already opened the front door to them and waited patiently for them to come inside, Alfie was really looking forward to the legendary gardens and going inside.

Then Alfie quickly realised that the female butler was not opening the little red front door for them but instead opening it for a very elderly man to stumble out.

Alfie, Louis and Penelope got out the Land Rover and Alfie was so relieved to smell the crisp, refreshing country air with hints of pine, peanuts and wood smoke mixing into the air that was sheer heaven, and the elderly man waved his fist at Louis.

"Get your car off my property," the elderly man said.

Alfie really focused on the idiot back in his black waistcoat, black dirty shoes and stupid pocket watch that was hanging out of his top pocket like he was some Victorian that hadn't realised the ages had changed.

"This is not *your* home, Secretary Of State," Penelope said firmly.

As soon as Penelope said it, Alfie realised exactly who it was and if Alfie had known he would be meeting a member of the government today then he would have dressed even worse than his skin-tight blue jeans, white shirt and white trainers.

If he was going to be investigating a bombsite he at least wanted to be comfortable.

"Lady Penelope," the elderly idiot said bowing his head slightly.

Alfie had no idea that was her official title, and it just went to show how normal the Pimples were as they rarely used their official titles unlike most pompous Lords and Ladies of the Realm.

"The car stays, and where is Mr Clutch," Penelope said raising her head high as she firmly knew she was in complete control of the situation now.

The female butler stepped forward. "He is in the Greenhouse Madame,"

"Thank you Ester," Penelope said.

Alfie was about to go towards the country manor as that was surely where they would go first after a four-hour drive but clearly that wasn't going to happen.

Penelope clicked her fingers and she started marching off on the multicoloured gravel driveway and presumably she was going to lead them round the back of the manor.

Alfie and Louis quickly followed.

A few minutes later, Alfie was amazed at the sheer expanse of the stunning rose, flower and vegetable garden that stretched on for kilometres with thick wide flower beds lining and creating patterns in the immense garden. Alfie wouldn't know for sure until he went into the manor and went to the third story but he was sure the flower beds created a breath-taking wheel-shaped pattern.

And right in the centre of the wheel-shaped garden design was a bombed-out something.

Alfie couldn't tell if it was a marble house, just an open-air altar or maybe even a mini-chapel, the bombing had destroyed it completely only leaving small shards of something on the ground inside a charred husk of its former self.

Alfie followed Penelope with Louis very close behind him as she led them through the delightfully scented garden with refreshing hints of roses, sweet-peas and rosemary filling the air. The sheer smell and look of the garden was like a symphony for the senses.

It was sensational.

When they eventually made it through the immense garden, Alfie knelt on the ground and could feel Louis's glaze burn his bum from he was staring at it so much but if Louis was doing the same then Alfie would hardly be doing anything different.

Then Alfie ran his fingers through the charred dirt as they inspected the bombsite that now Alfie was inside, he knew it was about twenty metres in diametre with a good chunk of flowers and beds destroyed too.

The only debris left inside the circle were smashed shards of marble, wood and glass that was covered in something sticky.

"What did the bomb techs find out?" Alfie asked.

Penelope folded her arms. "All we know for certain is the bombers placed the bomb under the open-air altar with white marble pillars around it, very romantic, and it accidentally exploded when the gardener came up here for a smoke,"

Alfie just shook his head. He always knew that smoking would kill people in the end.

"The gardener's family was paid a hundred thousand pounds for their loss but we still don't know how the bomb was placed here in the first place. There are two hundred security cameras on the estate and not a single one saw anything," Penelope said.

Alfie wasn't surprised. The Iranians might have been crazy but they weren't stupid so something else had to have happened.

"What if one of the staff members did it?" Louis asked. "Or the gardener himself?"

Penelope laughed. "Don't be silly. All the staff members have been serving us for twenty years at least, we pay them extremely well for their positions and they are part of the family,"

Alfie quickly understood what Louis was getting at.

"But how long was Alfred and his best friend friends for?" Alfie asked.

Penelope's smile only grew until it hit what Alfie was saying, because it was starting to become clear that the Iranian cell they were dealing with were clearly very effective.

They were able to turn Alfred's best friend of thirty years on Alfred very easily. That idea just scared Alfie more than he wanted to admit because it raised a very deadly question.

Who else could the Iranians turn on the Pimples?

CHAPTER 18

Louis hated the awkward silence that followed his idea about the gardener being behind it, and as amazing as an intelligence officer as Penelope was, unlike Louis he really doubted she had ever had a betrayal. Louis had been betrayed by a fellow agent very early on in his intelligence career so he knew the deadly consequences and how much it hurt.

"It's impossible," Penelope said weakly as if she was trying to convince herself more than them.

Louis wrapped an arm round Alfie's fit sexy body and kissed him on the head. The garden was completely amazing with its massive thick rose, flower and vegetable beds, and if they weren't in the middle of solving an international conspiracy Louis would seriously bring up the idea of getting married here.

Because the entire estate was so beautiful and perfect and really romantic. It was just perfect for Louis's beautiful man.

"What do you know about the gardener? What

about the family?" Louis asked.

Penelope looked round as if she was looking for a seat that was no longer here, or it was probably and it was just in shards now.

"I don't know. Frank had two daughters who grew up on the estate, I played with them as a teenager and we were all the best of friends. The two daughters went to university and studied…" Penelope said.

"What?" Alfie asked.

Louis took out his smartphone and looked up the names and recent activities of the Gardener Frank's two daughters.

"They both studied International Relations and, I think Mindy, studied Middle Eastern relations and visited the middle east," Penelope said.

Louis just shook his head as his phone showed him Mindy's passport being used to enter Iran for a seven-day visit two weeks ago but it was never scanned leaving.

Louis showed Alfie and Penelope his phone and Penelope just looked furious.

"Do you have the sister's number?" Alfie asked.

Penelope nodded, took out her smartphone and dialled it. Louis really hoped the sister could reveal what happened to Mindy.

Penelope put the phone on speaker and placed a finger over her lips as she looked at Louis and Alfie. They all knew to be quiet here.

"Hey Penny," Mindy's sister said, sounding a

little nervous.

"Hi Ruby," Penelope said. "Just trying to reach Mindy but I can't reach her. She wanted some career advice in the Home Office. Can you tell me where she is?"

Louis didn't like the silence on the other side of the phone and he could have sworn he even heard some whispering.

"Still there?" Penelope asked.

"Of course just had to take a sip of water you know like I used to when we went clubbing. It's odd she isn't answering her phone, I'll call at midnight for you and see what happens after the film bye,"

The line went dead.

Louis just smiled for some reason. "I have a feeling Ruby's a very smart woman,"

Penelope and Alfie nodded.

"Where did you two go clubbing? Anything ever happened at midnight and what film did you see together?" Alfie asked.

Penelope gestured them to start walking their way back to the country manor and Louis had no problem with that whatsoever, anything to see and smell more of those beautiful flowers again, and hopefully see Alfie's amazing ass move in those jeans.

But Louis had to settle as beautiful Alfie wrapped his arms round him as they went back to through the amazing wheel-shape garden.

"We only ever really went clubbing once in Soho. She was questioning herself at the time and wanted to meet some women so we went to… the Miss Marble Fairy,"

Louis and Alfie just rolled their eyes at each other, it was little wonder to Louis that poor Ruby who was clearly kidnapped had referred to that awful club. It pretended to be the poshest, most wonderful lesbian bar with a few special nights throughout the month but in reality it was so dirty and smelly and just disgusting.

"What about midnight?" Louis asked.

Penelope shrugged as she ran her hand down a row of rosemary bushes.

"I don't know. We didn't stay out late enough clubbing for that… but the night before she went to university I drove her down to London because her family couldn't the next day. I took her out for dinner that night and she *accidentally* kissed me,"

Louis loved it how Alfie's eyes widened at that bit.

"I didn't like it," Penelope said. "But she did and I made her promise me to explore her sexuality at university,"

"Where was the kiss?" Louis asked as they exited the immensely long row of flower beds and started going up the hill towards the country manor.

"Something in Bloomsbury," Penelope said.

Louis couldn't understand that, Bloomsbury was in a completely different part of London to Soho. Why was Ruby giving them completely different directions?

"And the film?" Alfie asked.

Penelope smiled. "It was with her sister. We all went to see a new superhero film back in the day but the two sisters were too young to see it so we snuck in instead,"

Louis smiled. That really did sound like the Penelope they all knew and loved.

"But that was close to St Pancras International the train station," Penelope said.

"That woman's amazing," Alfie said.

"What?" Louis asked.

"Ruby isn't giving us places to look for her," Alfie said. "She's given us three places Penelope knows of so we can triangulate her position,"

Wow that really was clever.

Penelope took out her phone. "I'll call MI5 and get them to search all houses in the area connected to Iran,"

Louis just hugged and kissed his beautiful fiancée.

But he couldn't deny that if the Iranian were willing to take people's adult children hostage to make the parents bend to their will.

Then Louis really couldn't be sure how far the Iranians would go to make sure all the Pimples were well and truly dead.

And what would they do to the people who got in their way?

CHAPTER 19

Alfie really wanted nothing more than to race back to London to start taking part in the search for Ruby in that very clever area of London that she had given them, but sadly Penelope, and Louis had backed her up, said that the four hour drive back to London was useless for now and they might as well stay the night.

As much as Alfie loved the country manor with its large ancient rooms, musky smelly history books and its excellent artwork, he really did just want to be in London working on the case.

But as he sat on a very large and long dark walnut dinner table from the 1800s in a longer and thicker room with dark black wooden beams running above them, ancient bookcases mounted into the walls and a roaring crackling fire next to them, Alfie supposed this wasn't the worst place to be.

And Penelope had been kind enough to have the servants make up a bed for them, but for now Alfie just stared into the dancing, twirling, swirling flames of the old fireplace as the darkness veiled the land outside.

"Why don't you turn off your laptop?" Louis asked moving closer to Alfie.

Alfie had left his laptop turned on with his emails open just in case the MI5 teams searching London found something or someone. Alfie seriously hoped they did, he didn't want to imagine what poor Ruby was suffering at the hands of the Iranians.

"We're working," Alfie said.

Louis took Alfie's hand and slowly started rubbing it, then he kissed it and Alfie just smiled. Because he was really starting to wonder how long it was until he asked to have sex on the ancient Victorian rug in front of the roaring fire.

Alfie actually wouldn't have minded that because it would be so romantic and perfect for them as a newly engaged couple but he still wanted to focus on work.

"You've done enough today," Louis said, moving his chair and resting his head on Alfie's shoulder.

Alfie kissed Louis on the head. "But we need to solve this, protect the Pimples and…. protect the country,"

"Are you only here for the promotion?" Louis asked.

Alfie was about to say yes because it was the truth. He really, really did love Penelope and the other members of the Pimple family but they were superspies, so they could handle the situation alone.

And if Alfred really cared about Alfie and wanted him to become a real intelligence officer again then he could make it happen without using the case as blackmail.

But there was something in Louis's voice that made Alfie really not want to confirm it outright. It was almost like Louis was going to judge him for focusing on the promotion.

"I'm here for our friend," Alfie said, which wasn't a complete lie.

Louis laughed a little and leant forward to poke at the burning logs a little more.

"Where should we get married?" Louis asked, resting his chin on Alfie's shoulder.

Alfie smiled and kissed him on the lips. He was really looking forward to getting married.

"I don't know. I'm not getting married in a church," Alfie said.

"Definitely," Louis said. "What about here or another country estate? It's beautiful,"

He was completely right about that, the Pimple estate was stunning and it really would be so romantic getting married in the middle of that wheel-shaped flower bed garden. But was that too much to ask Penelope?

Of course Penelope would go for it because Alfie just knew that she loved them both but he wasn't sure. And shouldn't they both forget about the wedding for a little bit and focus on the case?

They were working on saving the life of their best friend and her parents.

"Maybe," Alfie said. "It's beautiful and I do want to, it's just-"

Louis sat up perfectly straight. "You don't want to talk about the wedding, do you? You want to focus on the case and getting your revenge,"

Alfie's eyebrows rose, he had absolutely no clue what he was talking about.

"Don't look at me like that," Louis said. "The only reason you're here and with me at all is because you want your revenge over Sebastian,"

Alfie didn't want it to be true. He loved Louis. "I was the one that asked and wanted you to marry me. You didn't ask me. And Sebastian was awful. He deserves to suffer,"

Louis folded his arms. "If I didn't drive you here in *my* car and you came here alone. Would you be bothered that I wasn't?"

Alfie didn't get the question of course he wanted to come here to get the case done.

"Exactly," Louis said before laughing to himself.

"You didn't want me here or you only did when it helps you get your revenge," Louis said. "Is that all I am to you now since Alfred's job offer, a means to an end?"

Alfie wanted to shout and scream and protest at Louis for getting it completely wrong. All Alfie wanted to do was get the job promotion and make sure Sebastian got his punishment but he also knew that Louis was speaking a bit of truth.

Ever since the job offer he had barely thought about the wedding, wanting to spend the rest of his life with stunning Louis and moving on from Sebastian's damage. Instead all Alfie had been thinking about was the job promotion and seeing Sebastian suffer.

And it broke Alfie's heart that Louis had realised it before he had.

Louis stood up. "We didn't bring any clothes so I'm just leaving,"

Alfie reached for his arm but Louis pulled away.

"You know... I get what Sebastian did to you was crappy," Louis said. "But you at least could have seen I'm standing right in front of you. The man that loves you more than anything. I would die for you Alfie. But clearly that isn't enough,"

As Louis slammed the wooden door to the room shut, Alfie just raised his knees to his face, felt his voice womble and his eyes filled with water.

CHAPTER 20

All Louis wanted to do as he got back into his black Land Rover and just melted into its comfortably soft black seats and felt the coldness of the metal steering wheel was drive away and never see Alfie again, but Louis couldn't leave.

At least not yet anyway.

Louis could only see the faint lights of the country manor through the pitch darkness and presumably all the servants had pulled the curtains, so Louis just focused on a little light above the little red front door.

After all the things Louis had sacrificed for Alfie and given him, Louis just couldn't understand why Alfie was so obsessed with revenge. Louis had seen all the damage the newspapers and media reports had done to Alfie.

Louis had seen how the newspapers and media made Alfie out to be some gay slut that was a rubbish intelligence officer, a danger to the country and the worst hiring MI5 had ever made.

It was even worst that Sebastian had revealed classified details of MI5 operations that he had messed up and *not* Alfie, not that anyone cared about the truth.

Louis supposed the only reason why Sebastian hadn't been arrested under the Official Secrets Act was because MI5 choose to play the denial card, and arresting Sebastian would only confirm how true the reports were.

Something Louis partly understood.

But Louis had found, loved and supported Alfie for two years to help him get over it, Louis had showed him a level of love, respect and trust that no one ever had before according to Alfie.

Someone knocked on the passenger-side window.

Louis rolled his eyes when he saw it was Penelope in nothing but a blue silk nighty that was rather revealing, and she should have been resting with her getting married in two days time.

"Let me in please," Penelope said.

Louis rolled his eyes again and popped open the door and Penelope boarded the Land Rover.

"He said what he said," Louis said.

Penelope slowly nodded. "I know, he told me and I will say to you what I said to him,"

Louis really hoped this wasn't going to be another Pimple family-style drama.

"I was once helping MI6 and travelling across

mainland Europe by train and I was riding the Swiss Alps," Penelope said.

Louis couldn't believe she was actually allowed out of the country half the time.

"In the Swiss alps it gets very cold very fast and I had a massive crush on the MI6 agent I was with. He was beautiful. So me and him were in the dining cart when three Russians attacked us,"

Louis nodded just hoping there was relevancy at some point.

"So the rest of the dining cart ran away as me and my crush shot and killed the three Russians. I broke my leg and arm in the process and after the fighting was done, do you know what my MI6 crush did?"

"Kiss you?" Louis said.

"Na the bastard didn't," Penelope said. "He laughed at me saying he only bought me because he needed a meat shield to suffer instead of him. Then the bastard dumped me with my broken leg and arm off at the next stop,"

"Oh,"

"And let me tell you the Swiss are amazing but as soon as you tell them to contact MI6 they get very unfriendly," Penelope said.

Louis really hoped there was a lesson here because he seriously couldn't see one.

"My point is sometimes bad things happen and people betray us but we move on and find new loves,"

Louis just glared at her. "Are you seriously saying I've betrayed him?

"no no no," Penelope said. "I'm saying he needs to move on because, Louis, you really are a great guy. You loved and looked after my best friend when no one else would and I couldn't help him anymore,"

Louis smiled. "Maybe we both did worst jobs with him than we thought,"

Penelope gave a light laugh. "Maybe but... I understand why you're annoyed, and if you don't want to marry him anymore I can see why,"

Hearing that he might not want to marry Alfie anymore just felt like hammer blows against his chest. Louis couldn't imagine not marrying that beautiful sexy man but maybe Penelope was right.

Maybe Alfie was just too broken to see that Louis loved him, and as much as Louis did love him, did he really want to spend the rest of his life with someone that didn't appreciate him?

He actually didn't know the answer.

Penelope kissed him on the cheek. "Just come to the wedding please I need my two best friends,"

Louis looked at her properly in the little light that was provided by the light above the little red front door.

Penelope really did look beautiful and her fiancée was a lucky man, and Penelope was a great friend.

"Of course," Louis said. "Is there another house here or something please? I don't want to drive back to London angry and I really don't want Alfie to know I'm still here,"

"That is very clever my dear," Penelope said suddenly full of energy. "You know my great uncle died when he was driving angry. He just drove off a bridge like it was nobody's business,"

Louis didn't want to point out her great uncle committed suicide but clearly Penelope was happy still.

And as she smiled and laughed and told a few more Pimple family stories before finally telling him where there was another house he could park and stay in for the night, Louis just felt worse and worse.

He really did love amazing Alfie despite all his sexy flaws. But Louis wasn't sure in the slightest if he wanted to marry a man that didn't appreciate his love.

Louis always felt like coming to the Pimple country estate was a mistake and it broke his heart that he was right.

SPIES AND WEDDINGS

CHAPTER 21

Alfie just stared out the glass car window as Penelope drove him and her back to London in her very large black armoured SUV with bulletproof windows, machine guns mounted into the engine compartment and a lot of other tricks in case they were ever attacked, Alfie just watched the other cars in their different heights, sizes and colours drive past them on the motorway as all Alfie wanted to do was get back to London.

"How you feeling today?" Penelope asked like nothing was wrong in the entire world.

Alfie still hated it how Louis hadn't left last night like he said, he had only stayed in another small cottage on the property so clearly he wasn't as annoyed as he made out. But maybe Louis was just being smart and refusing to drive angrily, that was smart. If not a little annoying.

Alfie absolutely refused to believe that Louis was right about him, he was here to protect his best friend and the Pimple family, this wasn't some revenge or job promotion. It was all about protecting the innocent, something Alfie hadn't managed to do directly for ages.

The revenge and job promotion were great bonuses though, and Alfie really, really wanted them.

And in a way he really was just so typical of Louis to act up the way he was, Louis always acted up when Alfie didn't bend to his will or something.

"I'm fine," Alfie said.

So Alfie was definitely going to go after this job promotion, no matter what Louis believed because Alfie just wanted to be an intelligence officer again, even if that did put the wedding of his dreams at risk.

And he still desperately wanted to marry beautiful sexy Louis, Alfie just wanted it all in life.

Penelope laughed as her phone buzzed and Alfie answered it for her, putting it on speaker and thankfully it was someone from MI5.

"Ma'am," a young man said on the phone. "This is Captain White from Strike Team Beta we have found the girl,"

Alfie punched the air in delight that was really amazing news and finally they had their first solid lead, all without Louis's help.

"Captain," Penelope said. "Have the crime scene techs finished with the scene, is Ruby okay and are there any prisoners?"

The line went a little silent and Alfie just focused on a very large convoy of black SUVs coming down the motorway behind them.

"Negative," the Captain said. "The Iranians were very trigger happy but my team did send a bunch of laptops, phones and tablets to the lab for testing. The girl is okay but a little shaken. Do you want to talk to her when you return?"

"Yes please," Penelope said.

As much as Alfie wanted to focus on the conversation as the Captain started to talk about the results that the crime scene techs had from the house used to hold Ruby. He just couldn't help but look at the black convoy of SUVs that were gaining behind them.

"Penelope," Alfie said.

"Yes babe," Penelope said smiling.

"You know there's massive-" Alfie said.

Penelope spun a hard right.

Their SUV did a perfect 180.

Penelope floored it.

She was driving the wrong way on a motorway.

Penelope slammed her fists onto the dashboard.

Machine guns shot out of the car bonnet.

Penelope fired.

Alfie screamed as they raced towards the black SUVs.

The SUVs popped. Exploded. Bursted into flames.

An SUV rammed them.

Alfie flew forward. His seatbelt snapped.

More SUVs slammed into them.

Penelope pressed another button.

Engine oil poured onto the road.

Other cars honked their horns in terror.

Penelope reversed rapidly.

Alfie gripped onto the door handle.

Penelope's SUV raced down the motorway.

The engine oil got alight.

The black convoy of SUVs exploded in the distance.

Penelope activated their blue sirens.

Racing away.

Heading towards a massive concrete bridge with plenty of lorries on top.

Alfie seriously had no clue what had just happened but clearly someone wanted them dead.

The bridge ahead of them exploded.

CHAPTER 22

When Louis arrived back in London and went to MI5 and went into his sexy fiancée's office, the very last thing Louis expected was for it to be empty. Sure he had left a little sooner than beautiful Alfie and Penelope but it was weird they weren't back yet.

"Hello?" Wendy said, Penelope's receptionist, wearing her purple jumper, black trousers and very librarian-looking glasses.

Louis nodded his *hello* to her but as he went into Alfie's spacious office with its oak desk, large floor-to-ceiling windows and piles of intelligence reports on Alfie's desk. It was strange that they still weren't back.

And Louis just knew that something was very, very wrong. That's when he noticed Wendy was holding a very thick intelligence report folder that judging by the smell of drying ink that had printed a little too quickly.

Something very urgent was going on.

"What's in the report?" Louis asked.

Wendy popped her head into the office and looked around. "They should be back. I spoke to Captain White in the medical area and Penny and Al were heading back here,"

Louis really didn't like where this was going. Then he sort of snatched the report out of Wendy's hand.

Louis started reading it and it seemed to be the test results from the crime scene techs from the house that was holding Ruby. There were five Iranians holding her and they all died at the scene defending Ruby and keeping MI5 out. Nothing there was too surprising and the Iranian corpses were a dead end, literally.

The next bit of the report were the results from the computers, tablets and other pieces of tech that were taken in the raid. Louis was a bit surprised there were so many video chats found to Iran outside military and government channels which wasn't typical intelligence officer or Iranian behaviour whatsoever.

"My favourite part is the medical examination of Ruby," Wendy said.

And Louis really loved how she probably already knew everything in the report.

Louis flicked to the end of the very thick folder and was shocked to see there wasn't a single bruise, cut or injury on Ruby's body. Something that was flat out impossible unless a person didn't even try to escape from their captors.

Louis just looked at Wendy. "I'm guessing the doctors didn't find any sign of malnourishment or dehydration,"

Wendy smiled. "Of course not Pet,"

Louis liked it when Wendy went really common with him because it meant she trusted him, something Wendy didn't really do much at all of.

"In fact," Wendy said taking the folder and flicking to a miscellaneous section. "They found she had a lot of coffee, luxury middle eastern and even goat brain,"

Louis was shocked, that was completely not the sort of decadency the Iranians would have given a prisoner. Goat brain was only given to special people, like a friend or maybe even a leader.

Louis took out his smartphone and immediately dialled Captain White who was probably still with the medical team with Ruby.

The phone just came ringing.

"He won't answer," Wendy said. "He's dead,"

Louis didn't want to believe it so he just kept listening to the ringing.

Someone answered and just breathed down the phone.

"White if that's you stop Ruby. She is not a friend," Louis said.

A woman just laughed down the phone and said "A little too late,".

Louis seriously hated Ruby but then the news alerts on his phone buzzed something about an exploding bridge up tens of miles away from London.

As much as Louis just wanted to run to the medical area to stop Ruby he really felt the need to click on the news alert. He showed the alert and news article to Wendy as he read it.

It was something about a large concrete bridge had exploded because of lorries parked on it and there was a little black SUV trapped as tens of armoured men and women were approaching them.

The police and any other sort of help had yet to arrive.

"It's them," Louis said slowly.

He seriously couldn't handle the idea of beautiful Alfie and Penelope being in danger and it explained why they weren't back yet.

"Go!" Wendy shouted. "I'll call tactical support. Go to the helicopter pad and I'll get a chopper ready for you by the time you get there,"

Louis ran out the office.

"Get our people home!" Wendy shouted.

That was exactly what Louis planned to do and kill some fucking Iranians at the same time.

CHAPTER 23

Alfie couldn't believe it as he watched the massive concrete bridge ahead shatter like glass and come crashing down. Penelope slammed on the brakes but it was too late.

Their black SUV sped up towards the collapsing bridge and a massive chunk of concrete smashed down onto the engine bonnet and Alfie and Penelope shot out of the car.

Alfie and Penelope ran away from the black SUV just as it exploded and sent them flying through the air.

Alfie hated it as he hit the ground with a thud, his face smashing into the dirty motorway road and the only sound he heard was the ear-splitting ring that everyone suffered after being far too close to an explosion.

Alfie couldn't hear anything besides the ringing as he forced himself up and forced his senses not to focus on the awful outrageous smell of burning rubber, burning oil and smouldering wreckage from the concrete bridge and the lorries that caused the explosion in the first place.

Alfie couldn't see Penelope in the slightest and he really hoped she was okay and he hoped more than anything the annihilation of her car meant help was on the way.

In the distance Alfie saw a large convoy of bright red lorries drive down towards them with immense red snowploughs attached to the front.

As the lorries smashed into other cars filled with innocent people they flipped and smashed into other lanes on the motorway like they were nothing more than little toy cars.

Alfie just knew the lorries were filled with heavily armed foes so he had to escape but the now-destroyed concrete bridge was flaming in places and it was probably too unstable to climb over.

He couldn't escape that way.

Alfie couldn't jump over the railings in the central reservation and run onto the other lanes of the motorway. That was far too suicidal and deadly and just stupid.

Another dead end. Something he was about to be if he didn't think of something quickly.

Alfie quickly looked at the other railing that lined a small woodland area that lined all UK motorways these days and that was exactly where Alfie was going to have to run.

He ran towards the railing that separated him and

woodland.

Penelope tackled him to the ground.

Bullets smashed the ground around them.

Alfie still couldn't hear anything. He hated it. He really needed his hearing back.

A bullet smashed into Alfie's leg. He screamed but he could only feel the scream leave his throat.

Alfie watched as the red lorries smashed into more cars and stop and the sides of lorries dropped off.

Tens of heavily black armoured soldiers poured out. All armed with automatic rifles. They weren't Iranians but Alfie just knew they weren't friendly all the same.

Alfie looked at Penelope. She didn't look like she knew what to do either. They had to do something.

They didn't have any weapons. They didn't have anything. They only had each other.

But all Alfie wanted in that moment was the most beautiful man alive, his sexy sweet Louis who had given him so much and Alfie had been too stupid not to see it all sooner.

He was nothing without Louis, and Louis was nothing without him.

Another bullet smashed into Alfie's other leg. He screamed again.

His hearing returned and the sound of crackling flames, innocent people screaming out for help and the soldiers walking towards him smashed back him into like a tidal wave.

Alfie had to focus now. The soldiers were getting closer and they clearly didn't want to kill them so the aim was capture.

That meant there was time for Louis to save them and rescue them but Alfie had to help him.

Alfie subtly looked around for something like a bit of charcoal or something so he could write a note on the road describing the attackers or something.

He couldn't.

"You're coming with us," a heavily armed female soldier said grabbing Penelope.

Then a male soldier gripped Alfie by the throat and dragged him along too. Both Alfie and Penelope were being dragged towards the red lorries for some reason, Alfie wanted to fight but there was no point now.

Alfie was surprised when the soldiers dragged them past the massive red lorries and instead there was a small armoured truck waiting for them.

In the distance Alfie heard the sound of ten helicopters zooming towards them.

And he just smiled because help had arrived but he really didn't know if they were too late or not.

The soldiers smashed Alfie over the head and he went into a dreamless sleep.

CHAPTER 24

Louis had seriously forgotten how much he hated flying by helicopter with a passion but he pushed on because he absolutely had to save the amazing man he loved more than anything else in the world and the man he seriously wanted to marry.

Louis gripped a large metal bar just above the massive sliding door of the dark green Juno helicopter and stared out at the motorway below.

"Break formation," the pilot said.

Louis didn't exactly want to know what the pilots or the five soldiers acting as Louis's crew on each of the ten different Junos were thinking right now. He was a little more focused on the disgusting damage below with the smouldering concrete bridge, burning and flipped-over cars and all the injured people crawling across the road to try and get help.

Bullets screamed past the Junos.

Louis just focused on the group of bright red lorries that were parked near the smouldering concrete bridge with plenty of heavily armoured and armed black soldiers gathered at something smaller near the back of the group.

"Juno Squadron prepare for landing," Louis said.

The soldiers fired.

Two Junos exploded next to Louis.

He shielded his eyes. The soldiers were onto them.

Louis's Juno flew backwards. Bullets smashed into the hull. Denting its armour.

All the soldier crews on the Junos opened the sliding doors and grabbed onto something and aimed their automatic rifles.

Louis picked up his too and started aiming.

Juno banked hard left.

Louis almost fell out of the Juno. The helicopter shook violently.

Louis fired. Bullets flew towards the soldiers. Smashing into them.

Shattering their armour.

The group of soldiers started to move on the ground. They were up to something.

An enemy rocket roared through the air.

Annihilating a Juno like it was nothing.

Louis couldn't believe the enemy had rocket launchers. These people were flat out not messing about.

A black armoured truck zoomed away from the bright red lorries and soldiers.

"Follow that truck!" Louis shouted over the

noise of the shooting.

The pilot nodded.

Louis almost fell backwards as the Juno flew forward. They were gaining on the armoured truck.

The six other Junos flanked them.

More rockets roared through the air.

Some Junos missed the rockets. Others didn't.

Louis just wanted the pilot to go faster.

Someone kicked Louis's stomach. He almost fell out.

Bullets screamed around the cockpit.

The pilot's head exploded.

Louis spun around. There was a traitor soldier on board.

He had killed the four other soldiers.

The traitor slammed his fists into Louis.

Louis jumped forward.

Kicking the traitor.

The traitor caught Louis's leg. Swinging Louis towards the Juno's door.

Louis gripped a metal bar just above it. His legs dangling out of the Juno.

The pilot's corpse moved. Knocking the Juno controls.

The Juno spun out of control.

The traitor screamed. Being thrown out of the Juno.

The traitor grabbed Louis's legs. Louis kicked. Trying to shake the traitor free.

He wasn't moving.

Louis tried to swing his legs upwards. He couldn't.

The Juno spun more and more.

Louis couldn't see anything clearly. Everything was a blur.

Louis felt his legs shoot upwards.

The traitor screamed. His body slaughtered by the Juno's propellers.

They exploded. Sending deadly shards through the air.

The Juno started crashing.

The shards of propellers just missed Louis.

Louis couldn't see the ground. He didn't know how much longer he had left.

He heard a rope hit his face. He heard another Juno close.

Louis thought he heard shouting. He couldn't be sure.

The rope started to move away.

Louis grabbed the rope. Letting go of the Juno.

It smashed into the ground seconds later.

Louis just really hoped there weren't any more traitors within their ranks. He just had to save Alfie because Louis really, really needed to marry him.

And he didn't exactly want to marry a corpse.

CHAPTER 25

Alfie was seriously starting to lose his patience with these stupid, pathetic and traitorous soldiers that just had to be from some shady private security firm as he woke up handcuffed to a cold metal chair in the middle of a dark green armoured truck.

"We've got clearance to torture this one," a woman said.

Alfie really hated all the heavily armoured and armed soldiers in their black body armour that stared at him as he looked for a way out, of what was effectively a long dark green metal tube.

The sound of explosions, gunfire and rubber burning from outside gave Alfie little comfort because at least he knew help had arrived but it clearly wasn't being too effective.

So Alfie just focused on the thick square metal door at the end of the tube-like inside of the truck. That had to be his key to freedom but he couldn't see Penelope.

It was very unlikely they had killed her so Alfie had to escape and find her quickly before the Iranian masters of these idiot soldiers killed her.

Alfie really needed to buy himself time and hopefully slow the truck down so his help could arrive a little quicker than they were currently doing so.

"What's the plan for me?" Alfie asked. It was the best question he could think of with all the shooting outside going on.

The sound of bullets striking metal echoed around the inside. At least Alfie's help was managing to shoot the armoured truck.

A very short little woman carrying an automatic rifle stood up and walked over to Alfie. Alfie tried to move but pain shot through him because of the damn bullet wounds in his legs from earlier.

"We need to deliver you and Penelope to our masters, get paid and he can do whatever he wants with you," the woman said.

Alfie just smiled. After all his time he finally knew that the mastermind behind this Iranian cell was a master and Penelope was still onboard with the truck if they were going to be delivered together.

"Bastard!" Penelope shouted from behind Alfie.

Alfie forced himself to look round despite the minor strain it put on his legs and the pain it caused him. But there was only a solid steel wall behind him.

Alfie really wasn't impressed with the stupid of these soldiers.

"Did you seriously put her right next to the driver!" Alfie shouted.

The soldiers looked at the ground as they all realised what the hell they had just done.

"She's a Pimple!" Alfie shouted. "A superspy. Let me go now before she frees herself and kills us all in some road accident,"

All the soldiers looked at the short woman in front of Alfie. Alfie was rather scared that they were actually thinking of freeing him.

The woman slowly nodded and undid the handcuffs.

"Now!" Alfie shouted as loud as he could.

Nothing happened. All the soldiers just laughed.

"She can't free herself and-"

The truck jerked violently. Something from above smashed into the truck.

Alfie fell to one side. The truck felt like it was about to flip.

The truck straightened itself.

It drove faster.

Alfie dived forward.

Jumping onto the short woman. Pounding his fists into her.

Alfie felt the icy coldness of five rifle barrels pressed against his head.

A shot went off in the distance.

Alfie grabbed onto whatever he could. Penelope had freed herself. Shit was about to go down.

The truck spun a hard left.

The truck jerked.

The soldiers fell forward.

Alfie forced himself not to focus on the pain.

Soldiers smashed their armoured bodies into their peers on the other side of the tube.

Alfie jumped up. Snapping the neck of a soldier.

Alfie snatched his rifle.

The truck spun a hard right.

The truck flipped.

Alfie fired his rifles.

Bullets screamed through the air.

Bouncing off the walls.

Slicing into enemy bodies.

The truck landed with a thud. Landing the right way up.

The truck zoomed ahead.

Spinning a hard left.

The tyres exploded.

Bullets smashed above them.

The truck smashed into something. Coming to a stop.

Juno Helicopters landed nearby.

Alfie raised the rifle at the thick metal door.

The door exploded open. And Alfie collapsed to his knees as he saw the love of his life who was so happy to see Alfie was alive.

And Alfie was so happy to see sexy Louis in one piece but now they had a mission to finish.

CHAPTER 26

Louis seriously couldn't have been happier to get his best friend and the beautiful love of his life back safe and sound as they flew back to London on a Juno helicopter. The sound of propellers roared overhead despite them closing the black sliding doors and they all had to basically shout at each other as they sat closer to each other on the floor talking about the case.

Because they all knew they had to solve the case now. They couldn't waste time anymore especially with Penelope getting married tomorrow.

"I never expected Ruby to be a traitor," Penelope said.

Louis wrapped his arms round Alfie even more and kissed his head lightly. "I know but now Frank's part in the conspiracy is even stranger,"

"I disagree," Alfie shouted. "I think we've got this all wrong. I don't think this is about revenge strictly. I think this is about eliminating what the Pimples represent,"

Penelope leant closer.

"You're the best spies the UK has," Alfie shouted. "No other agents or family comes close to what you and your parents have achieved. If you die then the UK is horrifically weakened,"

Louis could only nod as the realisation of that sunk in. This wasn't about getting revenge for the death of a nuclear scientist, this was about putting Iran on the world stage as a spy-killing superpower.

Louis hated to imagine the sheer shockwave through the western and eastern intelligence community if the Pimples died. If Iran was the country to kill the Pimples then they would have China and Russia lining up to kiss their hands.

Iran would finally be a superpower because Russia and China and basically every single anti-UK power would be willing to give Iran whatever it wanted as a thank you. And the UK intelligence community wouldn't recover for decades.

That realisation terrified Louis.

"How does Amir, Ali and Ruby's family fit into?" Penelope asked.

"Amir from the photograph is probably from the Iranian government making sure the cell stays within mission guidelines and he probably isn't involved per se," Louis said.

Alfie nodded. "Ali has to be involved somehow because him and the two brothers who are also Amir's family are the only members we're certain that are apart of this cell,"

Penelope shook her head. "That's a lie actually.

We can also guess that Ruby and Mindy are part of the cell. It all fits with the fake kidnapping, they would know me and my family inside out and they would even know the classified routes I drive my SUV back to London. I drove those routes with them plenty of times,"

Louis just shook his head. As much as he didn't want to believe British-born people could become terrorists and work for the middle eastern powers he just knew it was an evil reality becoming realer and realer each day.

And Louis hardly would have been surprised if Mindy hadn't been recruited on her visits to Iran and they slowly worked on corrupting her sister.

The Juno shook a little as a strong gust of wind blew past.

"What about Frank?" Penelope asked.

Louis shrugged. "I doubt he was involved at all,"

"Agreed," Alfie shouted as the propellers got louder. "We know terror groups isolate their victims, they probably turned the daughters against Frank and then the daughters probably manipulated Frank into thinking they were in danger so he had to plant the bomb to save them,"

"And Frank made sure the bomb went off early to protect me," Penelope said looking at the floor.

Louis and Alfie nodded. It made perfect sense and from everything Louis had read about Frank it was exactly the sort of amazing friend he was to the Pimples.

Loyal to the end.

"But who's the leader?" Louis asked.

Alfie stood up hissing in agony and Louis had really missed looking at his amazing ass over the past day.

Alfie collapsed to the ground and Louis just held him as blood dripped out of Alfie's wounds. Thankfully MI5 had been given permission to trial a new superfast healing cream for intelligence officers so Louis just hoped when they returned to London it would work on Alfie.

Louis hated seeing the beautiful love of his life in pain.

But straight after they were healed and fixed and he loved Alfie, Louis just knew they absolutely had to hunt down Ruby and the other members of the cell before it was too late.

And with the wedding less than a day away.

They were seriously running out of time.

CHAPTER 27

Alfie's only real problem with MI5 was it always boasted itself on having all of the latest technology, equipment and gadgets that helped its agents save the UK again and again, but in reality, MI5's so-called sensational facial recognition software seriously needed some work.

Alfie, sexy Louis and Penelope stood in his large spacious office with the fiery setting sun sending bright orange light into it through the floor-to-ceiling windows, but just allowed his fingers to dance across the keyboard as he sat on his dark oak desk with Penelope and Louis sitting on the two blue fabric chairs in front of him.

He was currently running Ruby's and Mindy's faces through MI5's "best" facial recognition software that searched for them on social media, airport cameras and every single CCTV camera in the entire UK, because he was certain that Mindy had flown into the UK very recently.

"The video chats stopped two days ago," Louis said.

Alfie just nodded. It made perfect sense that Ruby was calling her sister in Iran for some reason and with their UK operation falling apart because Penelope phoned Ruby in the middle of something, Mindy flew to the UK.

And presumably her sister picked her up. All Alfie needed to do now was track down wherever the two terrorists went.

"Bodies are secured," Wendy said as she shuffled into the office with her horrible purple jumper as she went over to Penelope.

"Thank you Wendy," Penelope said. "Now go home and enjoy your evening. I'll pay you in full still,"

"Thank you ma'am," Wendy said hurrying out of the door.

"And make sure you're at my wedding!" Penelope shouted after her.

Alfie just looked at Louis briefly as he finished entering the commands for the search into the computer. He still felt so guilty about putting revenge and a job promotion ahead of Louis.

Louis really had done everything for him over the past two amazing years, Louis had loved Alfie when no one else would, and he even saw Alfie at his worst and still Louis wanted to marry him.

Alfie really knew he should have seen it sooner but Louis really was all he needed in life.

He didn't need to get revenge to be happy and he

certainly didn't need some job in Counterterrorism to be happy. He just needed the beautiful man sitting across from him, he needed Louis more than anything else in the entire world.

Alfie opened his mouth to tell sexy Louis that when his computer beeped and Penelope and Louis came to stand behind him.

Alfie was shocked that there was CCTV camera footage of Ruby and Mindy and the three other members of the cell entering a bright white building about ten minutes from here.

It was the same exact top-secret hospital building where Alfred was recovering from the gunshot.

Penelope whipped out her phone and dialled her mother.

No answer.

Alfie and Louis took out their phones and tried calling Alfred and his wife. Still no answer.

Alfie even called the hospital building itself and the phone didn't even ring.

"They must be blocking phone service in the building," Penelope said.

Damn it. This was not what Alfie wanted or needed at all. Then Alfie noticed that his phone service went out.

"Anyone got service?" Alfie asked.

The other two shook their heads.

A gunshot echoed from somewhere inside the building then Alfie heard the lift doors open and a body fell out.

The cold deadly sound of high-heels getting closer made Alfie, Louis and Penelope all whip out their guns, and Alfie just knew that Wendy, that amazing woman, was dead.

Alfie just fixed his gun on the very tall woman wearing a white silky robe, white Hijab that still showed her face and two pistols were in her hands.

Alfie couldn't believe that Mindy was here and she looked like she was ready to kill.

But as much as Alfie just wanted to kill her right there and then. He really knew that Penelope and Louis would have killed her already if they didn't want information first.

They still had to find that damn leader but Alfie just knew the longer they took with Mindy the higher the chance of Alfred being killed was.

But as Mindy raised her pistols aiming at Alfie's and Penelope's heads, Alfie realised there was no way in hell she was allowing them to leave alive.

CHAPTER 28

Louis seriously wanted nothing more in that moment to attack Mindy and rip out her throat for daring to attack or threaten his beautiful fiancée. It was outrageous that she was aiming the gun at Alfie.

So Louis went in front of Alfie and Mindy laughed.

"Allah would never allow you abominations to live," Mindy said.

"We can debate religious scripture all you want," Penelope said. "But why are you here?"

Mindy aimed the gun away from Penelope for a moment and shot out one of Alfie's wonderful floor-to-ceiling windows.

"I'm here to kill you once and for all then the Iranian revolution can begin. We can rise up and rebuild our glorious Persian empire in the name of Allah and finally burn down all you western bastards that dared to defy Allah's Will," Mindy said.

This was even worse than Louis ever thought

possible. He couldn't believe how someone could become so radicalised, no matter how many times he saw it happen again and again and again in the UK and around the world.

Yet it did make even more sense now why the Pimples had to die. Iran wanted real power, money and influence round the world but not just from China and Russia and other enemies of the west, but they clearly wanted to somehow unite the Middle East under Iran's banner and killing off the most famous intelligence officer family was a hell of a way to do it.

Louis took a few steps forward. He had to come up with a plan.

Then Mindy dropped her pistols and pulled off her silky robe revealing a suicide bomb filled with nails to maximise death attached to her body.

Louis really wanted to shoot her there and then but he noticed a small motion sensor on the bomb so if Mindy fell suddenly then the bomb would go off.

They weren't shooting Mindy that was for sure.

"A little insurance," Mindy said.

"This isn't martyrdom," Alfie said standing up.

Louis loved it how Alfie and Penelope came to stand in line with him like they were all truly unstoppable together. Because that's exactly what they were.

"Allah will not appreciate this," Penelope said with amazing conviction Louis almost believed it.

"She's right," Louis said. "Allah wants to Martyrs

to sacrifice themselves for his faithful worshippers. Allah is kind and wonderful and caring. If anything this acts dishonours his memory and everything Allah has tried to bring into this world,"

That wasn't a lie.

Mindy stamped her foot on the ground. "No! Allah loves me. He will take me. He will-"

"He will if you don't do this," Louis said.

Alfie took a few steps forward and Louis and Penelope followed him. Louis just hoped they all had a plan for when they reached Mindy.

"You have always been a good daughter to Allah," Penelope said. "Frank was so proud of you coming a Muslim. He respected your faith and loved you,"

"Liar!" Mindy shouted. "My father hated me,"

Mindy raised her hands like she was going to do something.

She started falling backwards.

Louis shot forward grabbing her.

Mindy punched Louis. Kicked him.

Mindy fell to the ground.

Louis fell on top of her.

Mindy laughed.

The bomb hissed. Hummed. Buzzed.

Louis shot up. Looked around.

Alfie had large black sofas on the other side of the office.

The three of them ran over to them.

Jumping behind them.

The bomb exploded.

Sending deadly shards of nails through the air.

The aroma of charred flesh filled the air. But no one cared.

Louis jumped up and grabbed Alfie searching him all over. Louis was relieved that his beautiful man was okay and alive. Louis kissed him a couple of times savouring the amazing feeling and taste of his lips.

"Lovers!" Penelope shouted running out of the office. "We have my father to save!"

Louis and Alfie both made sure their guns were loaded and they raced down the corridor hand in hand with Louis just hoping beyond hope that they could still save Alfred before it was all too late.

CHAPTER 29

Alfie was rather amazed as they entered a very long bright white corridor at the top-level of the top-secret hospital building that they hadn't seen a single member of the Iranian cell. They had sadly seen a lot of corpses and plenty of injured agents were hiding in their rooms just waiting for help to arrive.

But no sign of the Iranians yet.

Alfie carefully started walking down the long white corridor with sexy Louis and Penelope walking behind him. They all had their guns ready and loaded just in case they came across the enemy.

Which Alfie was fairly sure they would be coming across them very soon as Alfred's hospital room was only a few tens of metres away.

Alfie passed more and more wooden doors that offshoot into large hospital windows that Penelope and Louis searched so the Iranians couldn't ambush them.

But the weirdest thing about this corridor was

there wasn't an aroma of dead bodies, metallic vapourised blood or even the subtle undertone of guns being fired. There was always a smell after that had happened.

There was none of that here yet.

Alfie kept walking down the corridor and none of it was making sense because the Iranians should have been here and they would have killed someone by now. They had on all the other floors.

So why not on this one?

Alfie made it to the wooden door where Alfred was being kept and as Alfie walked in he was surprised that the hospital room was perfectly done.

Alfred was looking great with his muscles as he just stared with confusion as to why Alfie was in his room holding a gun. Alfred's hospital bed didn't look changed or strange and there wasn't a single thing out of place in the entire room.

Then Alfie noticed he couldn't hear the subtle beautiful breathing of Louis behind him anymore and his stomach flipped. He couldn't even hear Penelope's feet "subtly" walking down the corridor.

Alfie instantly went over to Alfred's bed and aimed the gun at the doorway.

"They're here," Alfie said.

Alfred huffed. "Where's my daughter?"

Gunshots went off.

Someone grabbed Alfie's feet.

Pulling him to the ground.

"Sorry," Alfred said.

Alfie's head hit the ground.

Ruby climbed on top of him.

Slamming her fists into Alfie's face.

Alfie tried to block.

Ruby was fast.

Alfred smacked Ruby in the back of the head.

Alfie kicked her. Throwing her off him.

Alfie jumped up.

A smelly man wrapped his hands round Alfie's throat.

Choking him. Alfie kicked. It didn't do anything.

Ruby got up. Punching Alfie in the stomach.

Harder and harder.

Pain flooded Alfie's senses.

Alfred got out of the bed.

Ruby jumped across the bed. Tackling Alfred.

Alfie jumped backwards.

The man holding him fell to the ground.

Alfie smashed his head into the man.

The man released him. Alfie saw the man was Ali.

Alfie kicked him in the head.

Ali screamed.

He heard Louis scream in pain.

Alfie's blood boiled. He couldn't have his fiancée injured.

Alfie jumped on Ali's head.

It cracked like an egg.

Ruby screamed.

She charged at Alfie.

Alfie spun around.

Ruby dived on him.

Throwing them both out into the corridor.

Penelope was fighting Amir.

Louis was fighting another man.

Ruby pressed her fingers into Alfie's throat.

Alfie gagged.

Alfie threw his weight to one side. Ruby punched him. It didn't do anything.

Ruby smashed Alfie's head into the floor. Pain flooded his senses.

Alfie's vision blurred. His lungs screamed for air.

Alfie briefly saw Alfred standing over him.

Ruby's corpse fell to the ground. Alfred had snapped her neck.

Alfie stood up and went to thank Alfred as Alfred collapsed to the ground and hissed in pain as his gunshot wounds opened up again.

A gun skidded past Alfie's feet. He looked at Penelope fighting Amir.

Alfie picked up the gun. Penelope saw it.

She jumped to the floor.

Alfie fired.

Shooting Amir in the head.

Penelope rushed over. Helping her father back into his hospital room.

Penelope had done a year of medical school. She might be able to save her father. Alfie really hoped so.

A man picked up Louis. Throwing him against the wall.

Alfie raised the gun. He fired.

No bullets came out.

The man pressed his foot on Louis's throat.

Alfie charged at the man.

Alfie jumped into the air.

Kicking the man in the head.

The man fell to the ground.

Alfie landed on top of him.

Alfie grabbed his head.

Smashing it into the ground.

Again and again.

"Leave my fucking fiancée alone!" Alfie shouted.

Even when the man's head was nothing more than a bloody sack of bones, blood and brain matter Alfie kept pounding the man's skull, who he now realised was one of Amir's brothers, against the ground until he felt Louis's strong sexy arms wrap round him.

"In here!" Penelope's mum shouted as she stormed into the corridor.

Alfie didn't even bother to smile or wave at them as he saw Penelope's mum storm the corridor with a tactical and medical team.

Alfie just fell back into Louis's arms and let the love of his life claim him because now Alfie truly understood at such a deep, deep level how much he loved Louis, and how badly he had treated Louis and even taken him for granted.

Alfie just hoped Louis could forgive him and they could find the leader of the Iranian cell.

As four members and Amir was now dead.

There were quickly running out of leads and the wedding was getting closer and closer.

CHAPTER 30

"Who the hell was that man I killed?" Alfie asked.

Louis absolutely knew that that was the most important question any of them had ever asked and as they all stood round Alfred's hospital bed as a male nurse with a rather great ass, not Alfie great but still great, tended to Alfred and healed him. Louis just knew that the single question they had to answer.

Louis kissed Alfie on the head as his beautiful fiancée clung to him like a sloth and as much as Louis loved having Alfie hug him so tight, he was a little concerned, but that just had to wait.

They had to find out who the hell that man was who Alfie had killed trying to save Louis.

"Well I have a story for this," Penelope said who looked so refreshed and renewed despite almost getting killed by Iranian terrorists.

"Not the time honey," Penelope's mother said firmly.

And Louis still had no idea how the hell the Pimples managed to look so beautiful and perfect and like nothing had ever happened to them after every single fight. Even Alfred looked perfectly well despite him having bullet wounds.

Penelope popped her head out of the hospital room. "Well facial recognition won't help us,"

Everyone laughed and Louis hugged Alfie even more. He really loved how protective Alfie was of him, and Louis him.

"Security cameras darling," Penelope's mother said.

Penelope took out her smartphone and presumably started searching for camera footage of the mystery man.

It had to be logical to presume that the mystery man was somehow connected to the Iranian cell. The man couldn't have been a member because Louis and the others had already learnt the identities of the five members, but Louis still couldn't understand why Amir had been here.

"What about Amir?" Louis asked.

Alfred nobly and royally waved his hand in the air. "Amir was always a little git. He was a foul traitor double-agent for the UK for years. It backfired but if anyone had enough money his loyalty could be bought,"

"Really?" Louis asked. "So it is possible he wasn't working for the Iranian government?"

"He most certainly was," Penelope's mother said.

"My sources confirmed he was in the country for Iranian Government business but I believe he was recruited and paid by the cell,"

"So the cell who work for the Iranian government paid a government operative to get involve with them against orders," Louis said. "That's suicide,"

"Suicide is a good risk when money's involved," Alfred said.

Louis could only agree. Money's how Louis had converted many assets over the years.

"Excuse me," the male nurse said with the great ass. "I'm not a spy but could the mystery man be someone sent to monitor the group by the leader?"

Louis supposed it was possible but like all intelligence games things were getting very complex, because Amir was supposedly sent by the Iranian government to monitor the cell's activity only to be turned by the cell so Amir served his own interests and not those of his government.

Or was it really as complex as he believed?

"I think you might be on to something," Louis said. "If we know anything about this cell it's how amazing they are at turning people,"

Alfie stood up straight but still made sure he was touching Louis, and Louis hardly had a problem with that.

"And would the leader of this cell really trust the five members to get the job done?" Alfie asked.

"Of course not," Penelope's mum said. "Not

with Ruby and Mindy being British-born and Amir being a turncoat tag along. I believe the leader has lost control of the group,"

"Here," Penelope said.

Louis had actually forgotten she was searching for the mystery man's face.

"I've run the man through facial recognition and I can affirm he is Amir-Ali a security officer working at the Iranian Embassy but there's an assassination notice on his head by the Iranian Government," Penelope said.

Louis clicked his fingers. "The cell went rogue,"

It was so cute watching Alfie nod next to him, Louis seriously loved him.

"I think the mission was just to get revenge for the nuclear scientist," Alfie said. "Then the cell must have gone further with the killing plan against Iran's wishes,"

"But the money for the private soldiers? The resources? And the rest?" Penelope asked.

Louis shrugged. "Maybe Iran did have a role in the later operation but I doubt it was the plan at first. Who is Amir-Ali connected to?"

Penelope's mother laughed. "Dearest O'Deal everyone in MI6 knows who Amir-Ali answers to these days,"

Louis and Alfie both stood up very straight.

"He answers to his father the Iranian Ambassador to the UK," Penelope's mother said.

"And we cannot just go and kill a country's

ambassador," Alfred said.

Alfie laughed. "Even if we can prove they're connected to a known terrorist and actively working with Amir-Ali,"

Louis just kissed that sexy man. Louis just knew the Iranians wouldn't bat an eyelid too seriously if their ambassador was a traitor to Iran and they still had to find and kill the last one of Amir's brothers.

The last surviving member of the Iranian cell.

But they had to do it quickly not just before the wedding celebrations started in full swing but before the Ambassador and the last Amir brother could escape the country.

Louis was just looking forward to finally killing the evil bastards that threatened everyone he loved.

CHAPTER 31

"Backup is ten minutes out," Penelope's mum said as she loaded her assault rifle.

Alfie still couldn't believe that both the amazing UK and dodgy Iranian governments had signed off on the hit three minutes ago. And now him, sexy Louis, Penelope and her mother were all racing towards a little private airport just outside London in their black SUV to stop the Iranian Ambassador and the last Amir brother from escaping.

Alfie gripped the SUV's cold door handle as Penelope hooked a sharp right and Alfie was shocked as they raced towards a black metal wire fence that was meant to act as some sort of gate.

The SUV went faster and faster. Alfie held his gun tightly in his hand as the metal gate got closer.

Alfie focused past the gate. There was a massive private concrete landing strip for private jets for the enemy to escape from with abandoned warehouses to Alfie's left and a large stream to Alfie's right.

There was nowhere else for the massive bright white private jet in the distance to go.

Alfie just knew that the Iranian Ambassador and the last Amir brother were going to have to escape, die or be captured. There was no other option for them.

Mainly because Alfie wasn't going to allow there to be.

The SUV smashed through the gate. Ripping the black metal wire fencing off its hinges.

The SUV raced towards the private jet.

Alfie and Louis opened their windows.

Alfie climbed out slightly. He aimed at the private jet. He fired.

His bullets screamed through the air.

Alfie noticed a small black car speeding towards the jet. Their targets hadn't boarded yet.

There was still some time.

The enemy SUV's engines popped.

Flames jumped out of the bonnet.

Penelope slammed on the brakes.

Everyone jumped out of the SUV.

Alfie ran as fast as he could.

The SUV exploded.

Throwing Alfie threw the air.

Alfie landed with a thud. He forced himself up.

He saw the private jet was lowering a ramp. Two dark figures were boarding.

Alfie jumped up. He ran towards the private jet.

Firing his gun.

His bullets smashed into the jet.

The two dark figures ran up the ramp.

The ramp closed.

Alfie ran faster.

Penelope joined him.

Penelope's mum fired her assault rifle.

The private jet hummed to life.

The cockpit windows shattered.

The pilots couldn't fly now.

Alfie aimed his gun at the pilots. He fired.

Flashes of light bounced around the cockpit.

A body fell out.

The private jet zoomed towards them.

Alfie looked around.

The private jet was heading for Louis.

Louis was standing there. Shooting. He wasn't moving.

Alfie charged at Louis.

The private jet got faster and faster.

Penelope and her mum kept firing.

One of the jet's engines exploded.

Alfie tackled Louis to the ground.

The private jet pulled to one side. Heading towards the large stream.

The jet's ramp lowered.

Penelope's mum shot at the last engines.

She exploded it.

Two dark figures jumped from the jet.

The jet smashed into the stream.

Alfie didn't waste any time. He ran straight for

the two dark figures.

The two figures jumped up. Firing assault rifles.

Alfie leapt to one side.

He realised the figures weren't shooting at him. They were shooting at Penelope and her mum.

Alfie got up. He watched Penelope spin around. Her body hitting the ground.

The same happened to her mum.

Alfie charged. He wasn't kidding around here.

He ran straight into one of the figures. It was the last Amir brother.

Alfie smashed his fists into his head. The brother didn't know what hit him.

Alfie broke his jaw. Broke his nose.

A man kicked Alfie in the head.

Knocking him to the ground.

Alfie felt someone climb on him.

The last Amir brother strangled Alfie.

Alfie gagged for air.

Alfie punched the brother in the throat.

The brother collapsed.

Alfie grabbed his gun. Shooting the brother in the head.

Alfie jumped up. Spun around. Saw the Iranian Ambassador pointing a gun at him.

Alfie fired but he didn't have any bullets left.

The Ambassador fired.

The bullet hit Alfie in the shoulder.

Alfie dived forward.

Tackling the ambassador.

The ambassador kicked Alfie in the head.

Pain flooded his senses.

Alfie collapsed to the ground.

Alfie saw the ambassador climb onto his chest. Pressing a knife against his throat.

Alfie tried to fight back. He couldn't. He was too weak.

Alfie heard footsteps run towards them.

The ambassador was distracted.

Alfie grabbed the knife. Twisted it in his hand.

Thrusting it into the ambassador's throat.

As dark rich red blood poured all over Alfie's face and the corpse fell onto him, Alfie forced himself through the immense pain from his shoulder to force the corpse off him.

Louis ran over and helped him up and Alfie just clung to him. Not because Louis had distracted his would-be killer long enough for Alfie to kill the ambassador first, but because he was so fed up with not being able to tell Louis exactly how he felt about him.

And not tell Louis how much he loved him so damn much.

Alfie kissed Louis and opened his mouth to tell him exactly how we felt when deafening sirens and helicopters and sound of army boots hitting concrete filled the air as their backup had arrived just a little too late.

And as Louis went to meet the army commander in charge of their backup and Alfie saw that Penelope and her mum were being helped up and escorted to a medevac helicopter he just knew that everyone was okay.

And no matter what happened tomorrow at the wedding, because it was Penelope after all of course there was still going to be a wedding, he was going to tell Louis exactly how he felt about him.

CHAPTER 32

The next day the amazing sound of wedding bells, live classical bands and harp players filled the absolutely amazingly rebuilt Pimple garden and Louis seriously loved it. Louis had no idea whatsoever how the Pimple family had managed to rebuild the stunning wheel-shaped garden with the large and wide rose, vegetable and flower beds that made the estate's garden look so stunning in Yorkshire, but they managed it.

And Louis really didn't care how, he was only interested in the stunning result.

Louis absolutely loved how sexy and beautiful Alfie looked in his black slightly-shiny wedding suit with his hair parted to the left, it made him look so cute and perfect and beautiful as the two of them sat on a long white marble bench with a number of other wedding guests at the front.

Louis had never really met Penelope's husband's parents so he was just assuming that the extremely proud 50-looking year olds were his parents in their amazing blue dress and blue suit. Louis really hoped his parents looked like that on his wedding day, if the wedding was still going ahead that was.

In front of Louis was a very good-looking replica of the white marble altar with marble pillars around the wedding group with Louis recognised plenty of top spies and different foreign friendly agents that the Pimples probably knew from all four corners of the Earth, and Louis even could have sworn he saw a few European Monarchs on the benches too.

As the harp players went solo, Louis just knew that the big event was about to happen and Penelope's rather gorgeous husband sort of jogged down the aisle. And Louis wasn't jealous at all when Alfie coughed and smiled because her husband was beautiful with his very tight and shiny black three-piece suit, freshly pressed handkerchief in his top pocket and white boots on his feet. He was definitely going traditional and he somehow managed to pull it off.

"I'm not dressing like that at our wedding," Alfie said.

Louis just smiled. That was one of the best things he ever could have wished to hear, after their arguments and the case Louis had seriously doubted Alfie still cared enough about him to marry him.

Louis was so, so glad he still did.

The harp players stopped and everyone stood up as the classical band played the absolute wedding classic *here comes the bride*, and then Penelope started to slowly walk down the aisle with a very slow moving Alfred coming down with her.

And Louis was just shocked at Penelope.

She had always been such a beautiful woman with her fit body, long blond hair and model-like face, but today of all days she really did look like an angel, a princess and the extreme personification of beauty in her long white flowing wedding dress.

She was just as beautiful as every single woman deserved to be on their wedding day.

As Penelope elegantly walked past, Louis and Alfie blew her both a kiss and she just smiled, and Louis understood why. It was really only the two of them and Penelope and her parents that truly understood how impossible it had been to get to this moment.

After all the terrorists, the bombings and the other trouble that the Iranian cell had caused them, the wedding of the year was finally happening to the best people Louis knew.

Penelope might have been chaotic, strange and an amazing intelligence officer at times with more bounties on her head than any other intelligence officer operating in the modern world, she was still an amazing friend at the end of the day, and she really, really did deserve happiness.

As the wedding ceremony went on and the vows were reading and everyone cried because of how beautiful it was, Louis was still amazed at the case that had delayed this most perfect of weddings.

He was amazed that Ruby had thought she really needed a backup plan in case she changed her mind about joining the Iranian cell, and when Alfie had worked that out very late last night, Louis completely agreed that it was the only explanation for why Ruby had led the team to her.

There was no better way to ensure Ruby was seen as an innocent to the cops if she had helped lead them to her, and when that failed Louis understood why she had ran and made sure to continue with the mission, because she must have realised there was no way back home.

Her only choice was to die fighting for something she wasn't even sure she believed in anymore.

Louis loved the feeling of Alfie's hand wrapped round his as Penelope's mother who was officiating the wedding announced Penelope and her husband as man and wife.

Everyone cheered, Louis's eyes teared up and slowly the happy couple slowly made their way down the aisle and back towards the house.

And Louis was so glad that the wedding had gone off without a hitch, because Penelope was amazing, he loved her and if anyone deserved a happily-ever-after it was definitely Penelope after everything she had done for the UK.

But Louis also knew that there was no reason for the wedding to have gone wrong now, because the threat from the Iranian cell was gone, Iran had promised the Pimples would be left alone and it turned out they had only sanctioned the hit for the ambassador because the UK had somehow managed to pressure them into signing the UK-Iran oil deal (and the Iranian government hated traitors) and it turned out the cell's ideology about rallying the middle east under Iran's banner wasn't actually that popular back in Iran.

So the cell had to go rogue in a way to prove the Iranian leadership wrong.

It was strange how the world worked out at times.

"Back to the main house now for drinks, photos and food!" Penelope's mother shouted.

Everyone started to walk away from the white marble benches and Louis was about to follow because he really didn't want to miss the speech that Alfred was meant to be making.

"Wait," Alfie said pulling on Louis's hand slightly.

Louis looked at the most beautiful man he had ever seen and was shocked when he saw Alfie go on one knee and smile at him.

Louis's stomach filled with butterflies, his hands turned sweaty and his head went light.

"Louis O'Deal," Alfie said. "I have been an ass to you. I have put my work and my revenge before you too many times, and I have taken your support, love and everything great about *you* for granted way more times than you deserve,"

Louis felt a lump form in his throat. He really hoped Alfie wasn't breaking up with him.

"I want you to know," Alfie said. "I was wrong. I was stupid. I was an idiot to ever treat you like that because you are the most amazing, special and kick-ass guy I have ever met, and I am so damn sorry for how I treated you,"

Louis felt dampness roll down his cheeks.

"I no longer care about Sebastian and what he did to me. I don't care about some job promotion. All I need is you. You are what I have always need so, Louis O'Deal, will you marry me?"

Louis laughed and cried and fell onto his knees and kissed the love of his life harder and harder.

Alfie laughed too and Louis loved how the two of them kissed. Their soft lips feeling amazing and special and exactly like they were the only two people in the entire world at that moment because they were truly the only two that did matter.

And Louis was so looking forward to finally marrying the love of his life and he just knew that their love was always going to burn forever, fiercely and passionately.

Because what they had was true love.

CHAPTER 33

Six months later, Alfie felt the most nervous he had ever been before as he stood in a makeshift white wooden marquee in the Pimple amazing wheel-shaped garden as he waited to marry the sexiest man he had ever met. There was no one else or anything in the white marquee, it was only a place to "hide" Alfie before Penelope's mother walked him down the aisle.

Alfie was amazingly glad that his parents were there sitting in the front row of white marble benches but they didn't feel exactly comfortable handing off their son to another man like he was a girl, Alfie was fine with that because they still loved him, and they had paid for the entire wedding.

So everything was fine.

Alfie listened to the classical live band that had also performed at Penelope's wedding, and as they played some sort of jazz cover (Louis's grand idea), Alfie just felt his stomach go tight then loose then fill with butterflies and then empty once more. His hands were completely sweaty and covered in little salt crystals but he was so looking forward to today.

The air was crisp, refreshing and just smelt of nature and Alfie just took that as a good sign that everything he had always wanted was about to happen, not because of the wedding tradition per se or the people here or anything that had happened in the build-up to the wedding.

But because he was always going to be with beautiful sexy Louis.

A few moments later, Penelope's mother walked in wearing a very beautiful ocean blue dress that made her look like a young woman in the cover of some top fashion magazine and her large baby pink hat really accented her entire look, and Alfie just knew that there was literally no one else he would rather have walking him down the aisle on his special day.

"You all ready?" Penelope's mum said.

"Am I meant to be this nervous?" Alfie asked smiling.

Penelope's mum just hugged him and Alfie had never seen her hug anyone before and then she kissed him on the cheek.

"Beautiful," Penelope's mum said firmly. "You are one of the most amazing gays I have ever met, you are a beautiful bride and you are going to be an amazing husband. You're going to go out there and knock them dead and me and Alfred have a surprise for you,"

Alfie almost didn't want to know what they had

planned for him as Alfie hooked his arm under Penelope's mother, and they both slowly stepped out of the bright white marquee.

As soon as Alfie and Penelope's mother started walking towards the short aisle made up of bright white marble benches with tons of their friends and family members looking beautiful in their dresses and suits as they stood up, waving at him, Alfie felt like his stomach was dancing and he seriously knew that this was right.

Penelope's mum led him down the aisle and Alfie realised that this was everything he had ever wanted since he was a little gay schoolboy. A beautiful wedding, a lot of amazing guests and… wow, a very beautiful husband.

Alfie saw Louis standing with his back to him by a large white marble altar, and even from the back of Louis Alfie was impressed.

Then Louis turned around and both their mouths opened and their faces lit up like they were two schoolboys who had just met for the very first time.

This was a moment that Alfie never wanted to end.

Louis's Italian suit was very expensive with a beautiful white silk shirt and tie that really accented the stunning colour of his sexy eyes and hair and his sensational schoolboy grin.

Penelope's mum gently released Alfie and he immediately went to Louis, and the two lovers definitely didn't need to be told to hold each other's hands.

Alfie loved the feeling of the sheer chemistry, love and utter affection flow between them. Then Penelope wearing a light purple dress came up and stood behind the altar, Alfie was so glad she was officiating the ceremony.

"Wait," Alfred said as he stood up from the front row of the white marble benches. "If the two grooms would allow me I have a surprise for you both,"

Alfie just smiled at Louis and they both nodded as they focused on Alfred.

Alfred bowed his head to them both. "Can Sebastian Crawford please stand up?"

Alfie was expecting himself to be mad that the Pimples had invited him of all people to their wedding, but he actually wasn't, Alfie was really glad that Sebastian was here to see that Alfie had never needed him and that Sebastian really was a pathetic loser.

He was even more surprised when Sebastian and Louie both wearing a black suit stood up. But it was great to see Louie was in full makeup and looking amazing in it.

"Sebastian Crawford," Alfred said. "I have been watching you for a long time, I have been watching you ever since you tried to destroy Alfie Steward's life and me and a number of agents have been gathering evidence on you,"

Alfie's mouth dropped when he saw Louie was taking out handcuffs.

Penelope's mum stepped forward. "Sebastian Crawford. You are being charged with treason, aiding terrorist activity as the information and ops you leaked lead to attacks against this country and most important I can confirm you will never see the light of day again,"

"What!" Sebastian shouted as Louie handcuffed him. "I'm your husband. I'm-"

"A traitor to this country and a damn plague on all of us," Louie said, deadly cold.

Alfie just smiled as Louie led Sebastian up towards the Pimple country manor where he noticed a very large group of men and women in black suits were standing ready to take Sebastian away forever.

Alfie couldn't believe that Sebastian was done for good and Alfie had finally gotten revenge he no longer needed, all because Alfred had kept his promise at all.

But had he kept both of them?

"And," Alfred said, "you notice even though Louie is head of Counterterrorism now there is still no head of Political and Global Affairs,"

Alfie just looked at Louis and realised that he really didn't care anymore. Six or seven months ago he really would have cared and done anything to get some lame job promotion but now he really didn't care.

Because he had everything he needed right in front of him.

And Alfred laughed and nodded as presumably

he suddenly understood why Alfie was looking at the man he truly, truly loved.

Alfie looked back at Alfred. "But I think Penelope would make a fine addition to Counterterrorism,"

Penelope gasped, but if there was anyone who Alfie wanted to have an extremely powerful and prestigious position in the UK and international intelligence community it would have to be his best friend.

"Only if you have my job," Penelope said.

Alfie just rubbed Louis's soft silky hands and he really didn't have a problem with that in the slightest, because with him working at MI5, he still got to see the love of his life every single day and that would still give him a chance to recover his career.

As Alfred agreed to everything and no one in the entire audience objected to any of it, Penelope started the ceremony and everyone's eyes filled with liquid. Alfie felt the sweat dripping down his back, his hands turned clammy and his stomach danced inside him.

And all Alfie could do was stare into the beautiful, sensational eyes of Louis, his now-husband, best friend and his soulmate.

Alfie never believed in soulmates before now, but now he was finally getting married to his, he truly did believe in love, soulmates and the sheer magical experience of finding the person he was meant to be with for the rest of his life.

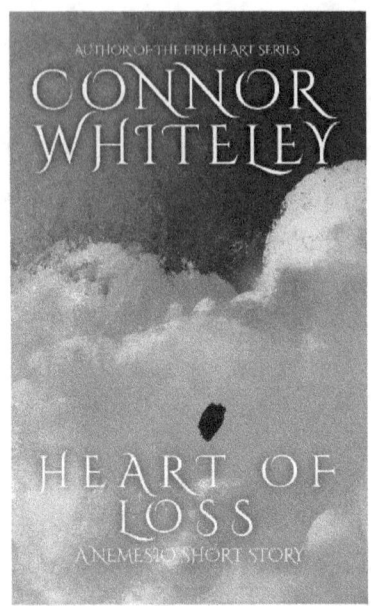

GET YOUR FREE AND EXCLUSIVE SHORT STORY NOW! LEARN ABOUT NEMESIO'S PAST!

https://www.subscribepage.com/fireheart

Keep up to date with exclusive deals on Connor Whiteley's Books, as well as the latest news about new releases and so much more!

Sign up for the Grab a Book and Chill Monthly newsletter, and you'll get one **FREE** ebook just for signing up: Agents of The Emperor Collection.

Sign Up Now!

https://dl.bookfunnel.com/f4p5xkprbk

About the author:

Connor Whiteley is the author of over 60 books in the sci-fi fantasy, nonfiction psychology and books for writer's genre and he is a Human Branding Speaker and Consultant.

He is a passionate warhammer 40,000 reader, psychology student and author.

Who narrates his own audiobooks and he hosts The Psychology World Podcast.

All whilst studying Psychology at the University of Kent, England.

Also, he was a former Explorer Scout where he gave a speech to the Maltese President in August 2018 and he attended Prince Charles' 70th Birthday Party at Buckingham Palace in May 2018.

Plus, he is a self-confessed coffee lover!

OTHER SHORT STORIES BY CONNOR WHITELEY

<u>Mystery Short Stories:</u>
Protecting The Woman She Hated
Finding A Royal Friend
Our Woman In Paris
Corrupt Driving
A Prime Assassination
Jubilee Thief
Jubilee, Terror, Celebrations
Negative Jubilation
Ghostly Jubilation
Killing For Womenkind
A Snowy Death
Miracle Of Death
A Spy In Rome
The 12:30 To St Pancreas
A Country In Trouble
A Smokey Way To Go
A Spicy Way To GO
A Marketing Way To Go
A Missing Way To Go
A Showering Way To Go
Poison In The Candy Cane
Christmas Innocence
You Better Watch Out
Christmas Theft

Trouble In Christmas
Smell of The Lake
Problem In A Car
Theft, Past and Team
Embezzler In The Room
A Strange Way To Go
A Horrible Way To Go
Ann Awful Way To Go
An Old Way To Go
A Fishy Way To Go
A Pointy Way To Go
A High Way To Go
A Fiery Way To Go
A Glassy Way To Go
A Chocolatey Way To Go
Kendra Detective Mystery Collection Volume 1
Kendra Detective Mystery Collection Volume 2
Stealing A Chance At Freedom
Glassblowing and Death
Theft of Independence
Cookie Thief
Marble Thief
Book Thief
Art Thief
Mated At The Morgue

The Big Five Whoopee Moments
Stealing An Election
Mystery Short Story Collection Volume 1
Mystery Short Story Collection Volume 2
Criminal Performance
Candy Detectives
Key To Birth In The Past

<u>Science Fiction Short Stories:</u>
Temptation
Superhuman Autospy
Blood In The Redwater
All Is Dust
Vigil
Emperor Forgive Us
Their Brave New World
Gummy Bear Detective
The Candy Detective
What Candies Fear
The Blurred Image
Shattered Legions
The First Rememberer
Life of A Rememberer
System of Wonder
Lifesaver
Remarkable Way She Died
The Interrogation of Annabella Stormic

Blade of The Emperor
Arbiter's Truth
Computation of Battle
Old One's Wrath
Puppets and Masters
Ship of Plague
Interrogation
Edge of Failure
One Way Choice
Acceptable Losses
Balance of Power
Good Idea At The Time
Escape Plan
Escape In The Hesitation
Inspiration In Need
Singing Warriors
Knowledge is Power
Killer of Polluters
Climate of Death
The Family Mailing Affair
Defining Criminality
The Martian Affair
A Cheating Affair
The Little Café Affair
Mountain of Death
Prisoner's Fight
Claws of Death

Bitter Air
Honey Hunt
Blade On A Train
<u>Fantasy Short Stories:</u>
City of Snow
City of Light
City of Vengeance
Dragons, Goats and Kingdom
Smog The Pathetic Dragon
Don't Go In The Shed
The Tomato Saver
The Remarkable Way She Died
The Bloodied Rose
Asmodia's Wrath
Heart of A Killer
Emissary of Blood
Dragon Coins
Dragon Tea
Dragon Rider
Sacrifice of the Soul
Heart of The Flesheater
Heart of The Regent
Heart of The Standing
Feline of The Lost
Heart of The Story
City of Fire
Awaiting Death

Other books by Connor Whiteley:

Bettie English Private Eye Series

A Very Private Woman

The Russian Case

A Very Urgent Matter

A Case Most Personal

Trains, Scots and Private Eyes

The Federation Protects

Lord of War Origin Trilogy:

Not Scared Of The Dark

Madness

Burn Them All

The Fireheart Fantasy Series

Heart of Fire

Heart of Lies

Heart of Prophecy

Heart of Bones

Heart of Fate

City of Assassins (Urban Fantasy)

City of Death

City of Marytrs

City of Pleasure

City of Power

<u>Agents of The Emperor</u>
Return of The Ancient Ones
Vigilance
Angels of Fire
Kingmaker
The Eight
The Lost Generation
<u>Lord Of War Trilogy (Agents of The Emperor)</u>
Not Scared Of The Dark
Madness
Burn It All Down

<u>The Garro Series- Fantasy/Sci-fi</u>
GARRO: GALAXY'S END
GARRO: RISE OF THE ORDER
GARRO: END TIMES
GARRO: SHORT STORIES
GARRO: COLLECTION
<u>GARRO: HERESY</u>
<u>GARRO: FAITHLESS</u>
<u>GARRO: DESTROYER OF WORLDS</u>
<u>GARRO: COLLECTIONS BOOK 4-6</u>
GARRO: MISTRESS OF BLOOD
GARRO: BEACON OF HOPE
GARRO: END OF DAYS

Winter Series- Fantasy Trilogy Books
WINTER'S COMING
WINTER'S HUNT
WINTER'S REVENGE
WINTER'S DISSENSION

Miscellaneous:
RETURN
FREEDOM
SALVATION
Reflection of Mount Flame
The Masked One
The Great Deer

Gay Romance Novellas
Breaking, Nursing, Repiaring A Broken Heart
Jacob And Daniel
Fallen For A Lie
Spying And Weddings

All books in 'An Introductory Series':
Careers In Psychology
Psychology of Suicide
Dementia Psychology
Forensic Psychology of Terrorism And Hostage-Taking
Forensic Psychology of False Allegations
Year In Psychology
BIOLOGICAL PSYCHOLOGY 3RD EDITION
COGNITIVE PSYCHOLOGY THIRD EDITION
SOCIAL PSYCHOLOGY- 3RD EDITION
ABNORMAL PSYCHOLOGY 3RD EDITION
PSYCHOLOGY OF RELATIONSHIPS- 3RD EDITION
DEVELOPMENTAL PSYCHOLOGY 3RD EDITION
HEALTH PSYCHOLOGY
RESEARCH IN PSYCHOLOGY
A GUIDE TO MENTAL HEALTH AND TREATMENT AROUND THE WORLD- A GLOBAL LOOK AT DEPRESSION
FORENSIC PSYCHOLOGY
THE FORENSIC PSYCHOLOGY OF THEFT, BURGLARY AND OTHER

CRIMES AGAINST PROPERTY
CRIMINAL PROFILING: A FORENSIC PSYCHOLOGY GUIDE TO FBI PROFILING AND GEOGRAPHICAL AND STATISTICAL PROFILING.
CLINICAL PSYCHOLOGY
FORMULATION IN PSYCHOTHERAPY
PERSONALITY PSYCHOLOGY AND INDIVIDUAL DIFFERENCES
CLINICAL PSYCHOLOGY REFLECTIONS VOLUME 1
CLINICAL PSYCHOLOGY REFLECTIONS VOLUME 2
Clinical Psychology Reflections Volume 3
CULT PSYCHOLOGY
Police Psychology

A Psychology Student's Guide To University
How Does University Work?
A Student's Guide To University And Learning
University Mental Health and Mindset

www.ingramcontent.com/pod-product-compliance
Lightning Source LLC
LaVergne TN
LVHW012106070526
838202LV00056B/5638